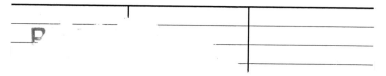

Calveron's Chase

After spending five years inside Redrock Stockade, the one-time US marshal Jackson Calveron sets out on a manhunt: travelling a gruelling 250 miles, across the border from Arizona to the New Mexico town of Las Cruces, to find the men who had him falsely accused, and convicted, of murder.

But when Jack finds himself involved in the aftermath of a brutal bank robbery, the death of a lone silver miner and the arrival of Fausto Salt and Copperhead Pintura, he begins to question his cause.

Lewis Berry has made a new life as town sheriff, and when his step-daughter Raphaela appears on the scene, Jack's mission is influenced by a new and more compelling sentiment. Retribution still awaits someone, but Jack has to decide who and what he is really fighting for.

Calveron's Chase

Caleb Rand

A Black Horse Western

ROBERT HALE · LONDON

ISBN 978-0-7198-1057-2

Robert Hale Limited
Clerkenwell House
Clerkenwell Green
London EC1R 0HT

www.halebooks.com

Typeset by
Derek Doyle & Associates, Shaw Heath
Printed and bound in Great Britain by
CPI Antony Rowe, Chippenham and Eastbourne

1

The horsemen clipped their mounts at an easy pace along the bustling main street of Las Cruces. Their attention shifted alternately from the flow of people along the raised walks to the traffic of wagons and buckboards, the ox carts and mule trains that trundled along the hard-packed dirt of the thoroughfare. The town was in overspill, bulging at the seams, and ripe as a peach for the picking.

The rail track that made its way up to the mountain town of Santa Rita, brought in regular shipments of gold and silver. Accordingly, stage lines from the south arrived with folk eager for work in the mines, or to set up businesses in Las Cruces itself. Cattlemen herded in their Texas beef, rubbing shoulders with miners as well as drummers and booze pedlars. The town had become a magnet, drawing settlers from as far east as the Mississippi Delta, Nebraska and Utah in the north. Men and women were pouring into Las Cruces in a steady stream . . . all raring to make their fortunes. Most of them came with honest intentions, but there were some who came to grab what they could, any way they could.

Fausto Salt rode point to the four men riding behind him. Now and again his mount would crow hop anxiously, breaking the flow of movement along the main street, causing it to shift away to either side. Salt was a man of heavy stature, his powerful shoulders were hunched, and his dark outfit was tattered and powdered with dust.

He looked directly ahead, or seemed to, with every sense alert. He was aware of the people who jostled along the walks, the resolute rolling creak of the vehicles, the blow of a steam engine in the new rail yard. He noted a hotel with a broad, white-painted veranda, a bath house, a two-storey mercantile. He smiled briefly at an older, false-fronted saloon with the unlikely name of Paraiso. Then there was a brick-built bank, a solid structure, with a uniformed, armed guard stationed at the entrance. The promising wealth of Las Cruces impressed Salt, and the corner of his mouth twitched into another tight smile.

Gethin Pintura now rode up alongside Salt. The consequence of a relationship between an immigrant Welsh pit worker and a full-blood Mescalero Apache, Pintura was barely a year out of his teens. He occasionally went by the dub of Copperhead, but that was a recognition more to do with the venomous qualities of a pit viper, the blackness of his eyes. Pintura was bemused by the array of stores and window displays that fronted the street, excited by ladies who lifted the hems of their skirts to cross the rutted stretches of roadway.

Salt was aware of Pintura's interests. The youngster was simply taking an imaginative romp with the town's attractions, and he wasn't unduly worried about it. He kept his attention on the road ahead. If he felt the pressure of keen eyes studying him from one of the boardwalks, he didn't let it show. He was used to the curiosity, the stares that went with it.

From the corner of his eye, he noted a tall, slope-shouldered man with a Colt that hung low and loose around his waist. He wasn't to know that the man was Goose Hollister, top railer and scout to Erskine Weaver, the man who was figuring on taking over Las Cruces, someday. But even if he had known, it wouldn't have made much difference: Salt was in town with a job to do, and he aimed to do it.

The grandly named Las Cruces Depository was tempting. Fausto Salt was a lot of disagreeable things, but blind stupid wasn't one of them. He wasn't for holding up a bank that had an armed guard outside just waiting for him. Work like that required a lot more support than he was currently riding with.

The three men behind Salt and Pintura weren't quite so imaginative, allowing their eyes and thoughts to loiter on more essential needs. Wallace Trench ran the back of his hand across his dry mouth as they rode past the next saloon. He ogled the painted sign of a beer glass topped with an inch of froth, his throat tasting like the dirt of the road beneath him.

Luther and Arlo Ring said nothing, though they exchanged glances and shared with Trench the need for a drink. They dragged their bleak eyes from the arresting sign and jogged in the wake of the men in front. Their hearts were small and as black as sin, and neither of them packed the courage of Salt, or the blaze of Pintura. The brothers had ridden from the north, where the climate of the law around Magdalena had become too warm and pressing. Now they aimed to get what they could in Las Cruces before hightailing for El Paso or the Arizona border.

Fausto Salt allowed himself a quiet, appreciative grunt as his eyes ran ahead to the canvas awning of the Santa Rita Development Bank. It was a small building that was once the Las Cruces claims and assay office. There was a hitching rail outside, though only one mount stood tethered. A yard at the side contained a rig and a horse that nosed tetchily at a patch of stubble grass.

A water trough stood near the hitching rail and a couple of ragamuffins who were splashing frantically, looked up. Their eyes narrowed guiltily, and they backed off, turning to run as Salt and Pintura dismounted.

Pintura didn't think it likely that such a scruffy young pair would be washing their hands and he went to take a closer look at the trough. Moments later he cursed, accepted that it was too late to save the small furry critter the youngsters had been drowning.

Flicking his reins loosely around the rail, Salt had

8

a quick glance back at the Ring brothers, then he nodded curtly at Trench and crossed the walkway. He paused briefly before stepping inside, then stood a moment longer while his eyes became accustomed to the light. He looked towards the teller's cage and the desk, the lone customer who was talking to a man in dark, corresponding waistcoat and trousers.

Both men glanced up as Salt entered. The smartly dressed man, immediately looked alarmed, darting a fearful eye at the teller, then back at the man he'd been in conversation with.

'If you've a mind to panic, go ahead. Just do it nice an' quiet,' Salt advised. His voice had a slightly hushed tone as though he was in church. 'We're here to make a little withdrawal, an' you all know how that's done. We won't make a fuss out o' this, an' as long as there's no surprises, none of us is goin' to get hurt.'

'They're robbing the bank,' the man gulped, as though he couldn't believe it. His spectacles slipped an inch down his nose with the run of sweat as he backed against the wall. There was a gun in an underside drawer of the desk, but at the moment he couldn't recall which one, and didn't dare go looking for it.

Salt had his arms folded across his chest. But behind him, Gethin Pintura pointed a long-barrelled Colt at the banker's head, while Wallace Trench waved his pistol to and fro at the others.

'As of right now we're short in this town o' yours,' Salt continued coolly. 'Mr helpful Teller there's goin'

9

to bag all the cash he can lay his hands on, an' then *you, sir*, will do the same with what's in the safe. Just keep tellin' yourselves, there won't be any trouble if you do it quickly an' quietly. Now, please get on with it.'

The banker had trouble speaking. 'Just do it,' he managed. 'Just do what he says.'

The teller took a heavy cloth bag from near his elbow and emptied a tray of silver coin into it. Then he stopped when Salt lifted a hand and shook his head in warning.

'I'm thinkin' on account of its weight, that stuff won't travel too well,' Salt levelled. 'So, notes only.'

The bank manager was as nervous and afraid as his solitary customer. The teller was too, but he also had a few guts to go with it. As he reached for the wads of banknotes, he diverted his hand into a narrow side compartment, located the shooter and drew it out.

Salt cursed and sidestepped. The gunshot flared in his face and a small calibre bullet thumped by his ear, burying itself in the wall close to Trench's head. Trench yelled and instinctively returned fire. The crash reverberated madly in the confines of the bank, and the bullet smashed fatally into the centre of the teller's chest.

'There's always one,' Salt rasped angrily, as he made a grab for the bagged cash. 'Now we'll have half the town down on us. Let's get out,' he yelled at the others.

Like a troubled hornets' nest, Las Cruces reacted to the sound of gunfire. Pintura turned and ran from the bank towards the tethered mounts. Ahead of him the sheriff and a deputy were already legging it from across the street. Someone with a shotgun emerged from a nearby alleyway, three or four others jostled for a closer look, braver in numbers and looking for something to blast away at.

Pintura grinned icily and put a bullet in the sheriff. He mouthed '*adios*' as the man fell, then fired again.

From the boardwalk, Salt quickly steadied himself, before dropping the deputy with a well-aimed shot to the head. 'Now's it's just everybody else we got to worry about,' he seethed, and made a grab for his mount.

Within a few more seconds they were racing their horses, kicking wildly for the outskirts of town, flight from the guns and impending wrath of its citizens.

2

Later that morning, two more men were riding to Las Cruces. But they weren't riding together.

Reb Fawcett was from Tucson, Arizona. He'd ridden west across the border to Lordsburg, around Cooks Peak, then south to the Malpais Lava Beds. He was a man who travelled with a lean and unforgiving shadow in his wake, a constant dread in his gut.

As he rode, his thoughts went over the same thing, again and again – the wish that he'd never let them talk him into it. They'd paid him to disappear, to give the impression he was dead. They claimed he'd been tossed in the Gila, his body carried away, lost down-river, way south of Picacho. Reb Fawcett was dead, and they alleged it was the US Marshal, Jackson Calveron who'd killed him. It was a feasible set up, contrived purposely to get Calveron out of the way. Hanged or imprisoned it didn't matter, only that the man was got rid of. It was only after Fawcett had skulked away to count his cash payment, that he fully realized that some day Calveron would be free to

12

come after him.

Now, Fawcett was on the run and he shuddered. He looked back, scanning the wind-blown trail. There was an ominous shadow following him, and he heeled the weary bronc. There would be no shaking free of the relentless pursuit. Calveron had served five years in Redrock Stockade, so he wasn't for giving up, ever abandoning the search. He would find Fawcett, drag him all the way back to the Tucson courtroom, living proof of an appalling injustice.

Fawcett hurried the mount, slapping reins along a neck darkly streaked with sweat. The wind had slackened slightly, though occasional eddies of dust still sprang up and scudded westward. Beneath him, quail and bobwhites ran for cover, quarrelling in the mesquite, killing time until he passed by.

He held his hand to shield his eyes against the glare, felt the first breaths of autumn disturb the pockets of heat as he rode on. Pure stands of bull pine mantled a ridge somewhere above the Rio Grande, and the San Andreas foothills appeared to be no further than a day's ride. But the distances were misleading and he had to press on, drive the horse until it buckled if need be.

Once in Las Cruces he could lose himself among the crowd, seek out Lewis Berry and explain the trouble that hounded him. Berry would help because he was one of those who had created the years of hell for Calveron.

Then, hard on the heels of wishing none of it had happened, another fear beset Fawcett – the possibility that Berry might have moved on from Las Cruces. There had been much talk of the Territory's riches, of Santa Rita and Mimbres, wealthy mountain towns that were growing in size to outrival Silver City and Las Cruces, itself. It could be that Berry was attracted by the lure of treasure, and had swung that way. Maybe he'd bought a ticket on the Pacific Flyer, gone far west to the diggings of California.

Fawcett's clothes were threadbare. His kneecaps showed through worn trousers, and his boots were cracked with holes in the soles. His eyes were red-rimmed and he ran his tongue across split, salt-crusted lips. It seemed everything was beginning to fail him, even his wits.

He saw weird and wonderful shapes in the spiralling dust-clouds. Roiling waves that were being eddied by the wind, flowing in broad, silvery ribbons. He saw snow-capped mountains, their lower slopes shimmering yellow and gold with aspen. A rainbow river coursed from the heights, blocks of melt ice bobbing in the fast-flowing current. Beavers grazed the bank, sizing up trees for their dam. A big mule deer looked up, backing off huffily when it saw Fawcett approaching.

Fawcett grated out a curse. 'Why pay hard-earned money for a bottle o' jimson juice?' he muttered as an exhausted, cynical thought. 'All this is free.' His chin dropped to his chest and he coughed, attempted a weary laugh. He checked his horse, unwound the lanyard of his canteen and drew a long pull. It was the fear that kept his mouth dry, the withered twist of rope that made up his inner vitals. How close was Calveron now? How much time did he have to get off the road and into a bunker or someone's fraidy hole? Hell, the nightmare was persistent, attacking his mind like a blue whistler. He was fatigued beyond measure, but he clung on, desperate to make Las Cruces and the help of Lewis Berry.

He blinked his eyes hard, staring ahead. He tried to penetrate the dust that was billowing up, fusing with the undersides of distant clouds. Now he was back to reality on a raw dirt trail, mountains looming, low hogbacks ahead, and a vengeful pursuant, behind.

Moments later, Fawcett head the noise, a drumming that grew louder. He kept his horse reined in as it too listened, pulling broadside across the trail. He couldn't tell from what direction the sound of running hoofs was coming – from all sides, everywhere it seemed, so great was his fear.

He reached for the old Navy Colt on his hip, fumbling to yank it clear. Panic was gripping him. Calveron had found him. It was over now, over and done.

The sounds became a pervading rumble in Fawcett's head. He drew the Colt, gripping it tight in a sweating palm as he raised his arm. *It's not him. It's not Calveron. There's more than one of 'em.* His mind screamed with relief as a bunch of riders came riding towards him.

The men were riding fast, urgently flailing their mounts, cursing and gesturing at one another. They came from the direction of Las Cruces, the border with New Mexico.

Fawcett slumped in the saddle. He let his gun hand drop, backing his horse two or three fearful, mesmerized steps. He heard the shouts as the men spotted him, watched dully as a big man in dark clothes raised a hand for them to hold up.

'Leave the son-of-a-bitch to me,' one of the other riders called out, raising the short barrel of a carbine.

'No. Christ, no,' Fawcett yelled. 'Don't shoot. I'm with you fellers . . . just goin' the other way, that's all.'

The second man riding towards Las Cruces that day was the one-time US Marshal Jackson Calveron. Like the man he hunted, Calveron was hunched forward in the saddle, sleepy and weakened by fatigue. The alkali dust had caked the sweat that soaked his clothes, stained the low-crowned Stetson he'd pulled down against the glare. He let his claybank mare travel at its own pace, rocking to a steady gait as it bore him onwards.

Calveron's face was lean, set determined. Beneath his dark hair, his eyes were the extraordinary colour of a mountain bluebird. In his stockinged feet he went a sturdy, fatless six foot. He was 250 miles travel-worn and it showed, but he'd journey a lot further to get his hands on the man named Reb Fawcett.

In Lordsburg and Cooks Peak he'd got close, and the disappointment of failure was great, with him constantly. Fawcett was ahead of him, riding with a purse of good fortune. But Calveron knew that that

16

sort of luck was invariably against the man who depended on it.

He was now riding through increasingly hard country. Mountains rose in the north and there were lava beds to the south, but he was heading east towards Las Cruces, where Fawcett was running to. From breaks in the low ridges of rock, wind caught at the dust and swirled it up into his face, but he just chewed at it, spitting sometimes. It was a lonesome trail he travelled, with only the gathering of bleak memories to encourage him. Another man might have given up, turned a cheek against the injustice and started over. But Jack Calveron wasn't going to do that; he was from a different kidney. When he'd pushed open the gates of the isolated stockade, he'd looked towards the rising sun and drawn a deep breath of fresh air. His job was to right a wrong, clear up the stain on his character. Only then would he be a free man.

The gunshot broke into Jack's bleak thoughts. The crack resounded flatly across the trail, merged to a jumble of smaller sounds as the echo of hoofs followed on. Then came the yelling and swearing of the riders.

They emerged from the dust, bunched together and driving their mounts as hard and fast as they could across the brutal terrain. A gun flashed from the swirling dust and Jack swayed sideways at the whine of a close bullet. He cursed, remembered the sneery warning of a Redrock night guard. 'Don't go east, jailbird. They don't want your sort,' he'd said.

'They've got 'emselves civilization.'

Jack had no more time for reflection as the riders came at him. He clawed hard at the reins, dug his heels in hard and, with a snort of alarm, the mare broke from its easy-going jog. He set the horse at a cleft between two low hogbacks, and it took the higher ground like a seasoned rim-rocker.

In the lee of an outcrop, Jack leapt from the saddle. He drew his big Colt, set its action as the riders bore down on him. 'Who the hell are you?' he hissed. 'Besides being too stupid to live.' He fired once, then again quickly. The Colt kicked in the palm of his hand, lumps of .44 calibre lead chewing lethally into the ferment of dust and riders. One of the men threw up his arms and arched backwards, then twisted down to the iron-hard dirt. Jack watched as he bounced, then stretched into a raggedy, lifeless heap. 'I hope your friends are watching,' he said icily.

But there were angry yells from the others, their guns rising in a frenzy of retaliation. They hauled and skidded their mounts around, came chasing back.

Jack took a deep, steadying breath. 'I used to specialize at this. Got paid for it too,' he grated, meting out two more reckoning shots.

One of the riders, a broad, darkly outfitted man, gasped, ducked low and cursed when he saw a bullet take a second member of his gang from the saddle.

'Goddamnit, what the hell do you want?' Jack yelled out. A bullet smacked across the crown of his hat, ramming it back and high across his forehead.

He closed his eyes for a moment, continued cursing as he removed the cylinder of his Colt.

'No one should have to suffer this sort o' welcoming party. Besides, I've paid a lot for what I didn't do.' Jack loaded six new cartridges. 'An' what happened to the civilization I was told so much about?' He licked his lips and spat drily, eased his spine firmly against the rock to face another charge.

3

The dull, cracking sound of gunfire echoed back and forth along the trail. The gang's leader shouted out some sort of command, then rowelled hard to get clear.

Jack Calveron held his Colt across his chest, peered through the whirling cloud of dust and gun-smoke. The fight was over as suddenly and unexpectedly as it had begun. He shook his head in bewilderment at what had just happened. 'Them who fights an' runs away,' he muttered. 'Must be some other place they've got to be.' He supposed the armed and hostile riders were being pursued, and obviously he'd stood in their way. At some cost, they'd cleared the hurdle, got past him to continue their panicky flight west.

Jack straightened up, took the reins of the mare and led it off the rocky step, back to the floor of the trail. The horse snorted as it neared the two dead men, and Jack quietened it with a few words. 'Just don't look,' he offered calmly.

He kneeled, turned the first man upwards towards the sun. It was a lean face, spare of just about any feature, and one that Jack was certain he'd never seen before. He turned away from the man's sightless eyes, looking in the direction of another bunch of approaching riders.

Coming from the direction of the border, the mounted bunch were keyed up, dragging to an excited halt as they spotted him. Some of them already held guns in outstretched arms.

'This isn't good,' Jack breathed, reaching up for his saddle scabbard and carbine.

'All o' you, hold fire. He's not one of 'em,' a leading rider shouted.

Jack immediately wondered who or what it was that he wasn't one of. But just as quick, realized what was meant.

The man issuing orders swung down from his sturdy chestnut mount. He wore a store suit, made dusty by the trail. His face was running with sweat and he was breathing hard from the exertion of his ride. He looked intently at Jack, then glanced quickly at each of the dead men. He took a calming breath, nodded as though to assure himself of what he saw. 'But these two turkeys are,' he said with a small grin.

Slowly, and so the man could see, Jack pushed his carbine back into its scabbard. From the cut of the riders, he assessed them as a hastily formed posse. They were all eager, a touch wild, but the man leading them had the authority of someone who knew what he was doing.

21

'I'm Leo Forge, Mayor Leo Forge,' Forge said and nodded curtly. 'Who are you?'

'Jack Calveron. The man who, for a moment thought he'd stepped back in time. You know, getting caught up with them crawfish who won't accept the war's over.'

'Yeah, I can imagine someone might think that. But it's not; they're bank robbers.' With that, Forge wheeled his horse and shouted at the posse. 'Don't sit there pullin' your goddamn pistols. Get after 'em before they get clear through to Arizona.'

With a thunder of hoofs, churning dust into the slowly clearing air, the posse rode off.

Forge watched them go as he drew a kerchief from his vest pocket. He dabbed at his face and around the inside of his collar, then he led his horse to the side of the trail, close to the rise of a hogback, and hunkered beside it. He was hot, uncomfortable and tetchy. 'If you ain't an undertaker or body robber who just happened by, I'm presumin' it was *you* done this killin', he charged, jabbing two fingers at the corpses. 'So, tell me feller, what the hell's goin' on?'

'The way they came at me, I had little choice but to defend myself. I didn't mean to kill 'em. I guess I'm not such a good shot as I used to be. Anyway, looks like you were intent on doing the same.'

'Yeah,' Forge nodded solemnly. 'Then I've got good reason.'

'It was your *money*, they took.'

'Some of it, yeah, from a bank in Las Cruces. They killed a teller an' a deputy. Put a bullet into the sheriff when they rode out. He'll live, but *they* won't. Not when we catch 'em. That's a mayor's bonus.'

Forge lapsed into a moment of silence, then his head lifted slightly. He read the miles of travel, the grim determination that was etched into Jack's weathered face. He met the pale-blue eyes, thought he saw answers to one or two questions.

'You don't look much like a gold digger, or a 'puncher or a whiskey salesman. So what is it brings *you* to this neck o' the woods?' he queried calmly.

'I'm looking for someone.'

'Here? Las Cruces?'

Jack shrugged. 'Could be. He was heading this way, and I wasn't too far behind him.'

Forge recalled the man sprawled across the trail nearer to town. A frown rippled across his forehead, showed itself in his eyes. 'Important to you is he, this someone?'

'Oh yeah, he's that all right,' Jack confirmed. 'An' I've travelled a ways to catch up with him.'

The concern remained with Forge. He got to his feet, dusted dirt from the seat of his trousers and grabbed at the reins of his horse. He swung into the saddle and nodded to Jack with a small motion of his head. 'Mount up,' he said. 'There's something you'd best take a look at.'

Something snatched Jack's vitals, stimulated a breeze of worry in his mind. He reached for the trailing reins, pulled the roan about in Forge's track. Forge edged his chestnut to one side and they rode on together, alert to the trail ahead.

'You've got the manner of a lawman,' Forge remarked, sort of casually. 'Maybe it's your reason for hunting this feller?'

Jack shrugged. He hardly ever spoke of why he hunted Reb Fawcett. Considering where he'd been, and the company he'd been keeping, there'd been no point in sharing that sort of confidence. But it wasn't a secret.

'I did five years in Redrock Stockade on account of Reb Fawcett. *That's* why I'm hunting him,' he said. 'Five years on a manslaughter charge, trumped up by a bunch of thieves who alleged I pitched the miserable son-of-a-bitch into the Gila.'

'So you aim to ride him down an' kill him.' Forge nodded an answer to his own question.

'No. I take him back. Killing would be quick and painless. Well, it wouldn't have to be quick or painless, but it wouldn't really prove my innocence.'

'Yeah, I understand. But suppose something's happened to this Reb Fawcett?' Forge gave a quick glance towards Jack, then back to the trail ahead. 'Five years is a long time. Suppose he's in some other lockup . . . saddling a cloud somewhere?'

Irritated, Jack gripped the reins tighter, stared across at Forge. 'I just told you, I've trailed him here,' he answered robustly. 'Unless you know something I don't?'

Forge gave a half smile, a half shake of the head. 'What I'm saying is, if he was dead, your work would be finished.'

'What's that to you?'

'You'd be at a loose end, an' right now, Las Cruces is short of a deputy sheriff.'

'Hell, you're getting a bit ahead of yourself.'

'Maybe. But I didn't get to be mayor by bein' one step behind.' Forge licked his lips while he considered what to say next. 'There was another feller. He looked to be aiming for Las Cruces too. Only he didn't fare so well.'

Jack pulled his mare to a halt, Forge's words banging at him like a hammer blow. 'Goddamnit, you're taking me to see Fawcett's body? It was those riders who killed him? The ones you're chasing? That's it, isn't it?'

'Partly. Maybe it ain't him; maybe it's some other poor bindle,' Forge suggested. 'An' maybe he ain't dead. He wasn't moving around too much, but we didn't stop to check if he was alive. We kept up the chase.'

Jack wasn't really taking in Leo Forge's last words. The banging was getting louder, a chill gripping his stomach. No, it can't be him, he thought. Not after I've followed him so far . . . don't let it be him.

'I'm not riding shotgun to a goddamn hospital wagon.' Forge sounded as if he was touched by a sudden twinge of guilt.

'Not so long ago, I was advised you had civilization out here,' Jack said.

'You were misinformed . . . badly,' Forge returned, with a crooked smile.

Jack cursed, dug his heels and the claybank snorted with a muscular lunge forward.

'Steady up, feller. He ain't going anywhere,' Forge yelled, urging his own mount to follow.

4

For ten minutes, the west-east trail twisted and turned its way further towards Las Cruces. Jack sent the mare close to the shoulder of a rising hogback, dragging on the reins as he sighted the lone mount ahead. Someone lay in the hard dust, face down and twisted, abandoned like a child's rag doll.

The mare pulled to a blowing halt and Jack hit the dirt. He ran forward, staring at the crumpled figure. With his insides full of curses and a thumping heart, he stooped to turn the limp form on to its back. He looked at the grimy face, the trickle of blood that had already thickened around a sagging mouth.

A single bullet had taken Reb Fawcett. It was drilled into his chest, lodged deep in his lungs.

Swearing aloud, Jack took hold of the narrow shoulders and shook. 'Goddamnit, Fawcett, don't go dead on me now. Do you know who I am?' he rasped. Cloudy eyes blinked up at him and he pushed the dying man's hat aside, lifted his head with a fistful of lank hair. 'Don't fool yourself into thinking you can

27

cheat me now, you son-of-a-bitch,' he muttered fiercely.

Leo Forge had caught up. Looking around him cautiously he drew rein and swung down. Then he walked forward quietly, watching and listening.

'You're coming back with me, Fawcett,' Jack held on determinedly. 'I'm Jack Calveron. You remember?'

Fawcett's throat constricted as words formed, coughed painfully with a gobbet of fresh blood. 'End o' my rope. Gave you a good run.'

'There's a doctor in Las Cruces. He'll take that lead out of you,' Jack said. 'Then it's back to Tucson and the Redrock Infirmary. You'll like it there.'

The shadow of a smile haunted Fawcett's lips. 'It's over, Calveron . . . was for you . . . now me. I ain't goin' anywhere.' The dying man shivered and groaned, and Jack's fingers gripped more tightly at his scalp, twisting.

'Where are the others? Where did they slither off to? Tell me, Fawcett, or I'll rip your goddamn head off.'

'Gallantree's dead.'

'There were six of you,' Jack replied anxiously. The proof he'd wanted was literally within his grasp. But there were five other men involved in the frame-up, and if he could nail just one, he'd get the confession. Six men had filed into the Tucson courtroom, placed willing hands on the Bible and swore lies against him. Was there anyone else with Gallantree, waiting outside the door of some hellhole for Fawcett to

28

join them?

'It's *them* I want, Reb. It never was you. I wanted you to lead me to 'em,' Jack lied. He shook Fawcett's head from side to side. 'Tell me where it hurts, Reb?' he asked with sham concern.

'Everywhere, Jack. Like a grizzler bustin' his way out.'

Jack placed the fingers of his free hand against Fawcett's chest, where blood from the wound had welled darkly. 'That'll be just here then,' he said and pressed hard. 'You were going to meet up with someone in Las Cruces. That's the truth isn't it, Reb? I'm sure not telling me makes the pain worse.'

Fawcett gave an agonized gasp, then a cough. Fresh blood rushed to his mouth, and his eyes rolled back until only the bloodshot whites showed. A shudder passed through Fawcett's whole body and Jack felt it in his fingers.

'Your life's on the move, Fawcett. It's leavin' you, an' I can't say I blame it.' Jack let go of the dead man's head, let his body fall to the ground. 'So thanks for nothing.'

Forge swallowed hard and cleared his throat. 'There's some hard bark on you, feller,' he said in amazement. 'Too bad you have to go back empty-handed.'

Jack's fists clenched until the bones of his knuckles showed. That Reb Fawcett had to die here at the hands of men he'd had no dealings with, was mocking reward. It was a cruel twist of fate, and bitterly disappointing. 'Yeah, that's right,' he conceded.

'As I said, it doesn't help prove my innocence.'

'I'm sorry. But if you hadn't rough-housed him, we might have got him back to town,' Forge offered tentatively.

'No you wouldn't,' Jack assured him. 'Besides, what the hell. That was my bonus.' He stared at Forge as though testing for a response. He moved to his mare, and stroked its forehead, led it close to the shade of the hogback.

'Being mayor o' Las Cruces doesn't mean much. Except two or three times a year, maybe.' Forge spoke as though his town standing was of little consequence. Nevertheless, he hoped it was enough to influence Jack. 'I told you we needed a new deputy, an' I'll say it again. We need a new deputy. Will you consider the job?'

Jack looked at him without speaking, so Forge went on quickly to press the proposition. 'I've put my cards on the table, but you obviously want to know the thinking. Well, you look like a man who can handle himself. I can vouch for your *feeling* for the work, but somethin' else tells me you know the law. Las Cruces is a big town an' booming, like its sisters, Santa Rita and Mimbres. We've got to have law an' order or we're in trouble. That's about the meat of it. Take the job for ninety dollars a month, all found. That's about three times what a cow waddy makes. Maybe it'll go some way to ease your anger . . . your regret. Wait until you get scrubbed up an' fed. See how you feel then?'

'Some of that mountain silver must've chafed your

tongue, Mr Mayor. Your way of putting things has taken me from no to a maybe to—' Jack stopped talking. He was looking past Forge to where the posse were riding back.

For a moment or two, both men watched silently as the weary riders shoved their mounts around the body of Reb Fawcett.

'Leo.' One of the men backed away from the others and confronted Forge. 'The trail's poor an' there's no sign. They gave us the slip, so what do we do? You figure we should scout around, try an' pick up their track again?'

Forge gave Jack a knowing look, a faint, tired smile. 'No. I doubt they'll come back to give you a second bite,' he said. 'They'll be halfway up the Mogollons. Besides, we've got the little matter of three corpses to dispose of. We'd best head back to town.'

As the rider wheeled away, shouting instructions to the others, Forge sided his chestnut closer to Jack. 'No need to say anything to the men . . . to anyone,' he said quietly. 'They don't need to know our business.'

'Thanks.' Jack managed a grin, albeit non-committal in return. He was thinking that Forge looked like a man who'd been softened by town living, indulging himself more than the two or three times a year that was mentioned. But he also saw toughness in the mayor, a thinking man and shrewd in business.

'Las Cruces is a tough town, don't get me wrong. Like its commercial wheeling an' dealing, there's more of it every passing day,' Forge went on in words that were measured, barely a murmur. 'What I'm saying, Jack, is if you were to take the job, there'd be enough action for you to work out on. But if that's not it, remember there's another side to the hill. If you decide you just want to start over, why not here?'

Nearing the San Andres foothills, Fausto Salt pulled his blowing mount to a halt, threw a long and searching look over his shoulder. Gethin Pintura drew rein beside him, and Wallace Trench stood off a few yards behind.

'They won't catch us now.' Salt spat into the dust, took a canteen and tilted it thirstily to his mouth. He took a long pull, punched the cap back in and re-tied it to the cantle of his saddle. 'Why did that goddamn cash-monger try an' be the hero? We could've cleaned the joint out. What the hell was it to him?' he said, irately.

'Yeah, well, he won't be there next time.' Pintura removed his hat, ran his fingers through damp, long hair, now even darker with sweat. He levelled an intense gaze on Salt and grinned.

'That's right, Gethin, 'cause there *will* be a next time,' Salt agreed. 'An' there'll be no slip ups next time. We'll ride in separately, get us a room and lie low a few days, look the town over, recruit more men if we have to. Maybe we'll take a crack at that fancy Las Cruces Depository. There must be a way in.'

'It's the way *out* that bothers me.' Pintura laughed at the thought, but not with derision or any disrespect.

In his eyes, Fausto Salt could do just about anything he set his mind to. If the man suggested they steal the Comstock Lode, they'd probably all agree.

'Yeah, that's where the *real* plannin' comes in. It was tough losin' the Ring boys.' Trench looked to the east, then eased himself from the saddle, dropped down to stretch his arms and legs. 'That stranger we ran up against was one hell of a marksman. That, or he got lucky. I can still hear that slug buzzin' by.'

Salt dismissed the men's reflections with a shrug, but he had already given more than a thought to the man they had gone up against back on the trail. He bit the end off a stogie, lit up and tasted the cheap smoke. He nodded at Pintura. 'We'll get out, an' all the richer for it. Place like Las Cruces, there'll be plenty o' hooters eager to throw in with us.'

At a steadier pace now, they rode on, climbing watchfully towards the timberline, off the top of the hogback into stands of bull and stunt pine. When they came to a small creek, Salt gave the order to dismount. They were still within riding distance of Las Cruces and with a lot of daylight remaining. But Salt was in no hurry. He wanted the dark, lessen the chances of being seen.

By nightfall most townsfolk of Las Cruces would have forgotten the excitement of the bank robbery, the saloons would be stirring up new thrills and pleasures of their own.

They watered the horses, slipped the saddles free and made coldharbour camp where grass was edging the bankside.

Salt sat with his back against a stump and closed his eyes. But his drowsing was soon broken by the sounds of Trench and Pintura shouting rowdily as they kneeled in the shallows. He shook his head when Pintura scooped water in his direction. Yeah, smart, he thought as it failed to reach him. Smart move.

The alliance between Salt and Pintura had been formed in Colorado. They'd ridden along the Rio Grande into New Mexico, then further south to Albuquerque and Magdalena. It was there that Wallace Trench and the Ring brothers had joined up with them. Trench was a good man to have along, but didn't share the regard that Salt allowed Gethin Pintura.

Pintura was blustering and laughing as he relished the chill bite of the water.

Ha, reminds me o' someone. Someone with the years removed, Salt was thinking.

'Hey Fausto, what's on your mind?' Pintura called out, noticing Salt's close attention.

Salt got to his feet and winced, paced back and forth a moment. 'Just seein' you in the water, the way that mane o' yours is off your face. It sort of made you look different . . . gave me an idea.'

Trench came out of the shallow stream, slapping his arms and stamping to get warm. 'Looks like our leader's suddenly got himself a heifer branded,' he said and guffawed crudely.

Save for the withering stab of a scowl, Salt ignored Trench's insinuation, returned to the study of

Pintura's features. 'Gethin, how'd you like to have your hair cut?' he asked levelly.

'An' how would you like me to hack your gonads off?' Pintura retorted quickly.

'Seriously. Calm down. Look upon it as savin' yourself fifty cents. That's the price of a wash an' brush-up in Las Cruces.' Salt stepped nearer, took a handful of Pintura's hair and dragged it tight back from his face. 'This ain't as foolish as it sounds.'

While the doubtful Pintura began to protest, Salt nodded in stern approval. 'Yeah, under all this facial stuff you've got the mug of a regular angel,' he said.

The mixed-blood youngster was blade keen, showed little reluctance to kill man or beast. The fire of the black eyes would remain, but shorn of the long dark hair and stubble, Salt saw something else in Gethin Pintura's face. A plan was beginning to unfold.

5

It was approaching first dark when Jack Calveron rode into the bustling main street of Las Cruces. Leo Forge was at his side, and the posse was single tracking behind them. As they jogged past a number of busy stores and workshops, Forge shook his head, frowned quizzically.

'What's wrong. You look puzzled?' Jack asked.

'I am. You remember I told you about the town growing fast . . . too fast?'

'Yeah, I remember.'

'Well, I swear some o' these businesses weren't here when I rode out,' he answered inscrutably.

Jack smiled. 'Perhaps a lawman's pay should go up as fast.'

They continued on by a livery where Forge called a halt, swivelling in his saddle to instruct the posse. 'You men can get back to your business. I'll get word to you if I need you again.'

Jack watched the posse break away. He guessed a few would head for a saloon, others presumably would ride to their homes.

Quite a few of Las Cruces citizens weren't so habitually active and stimulated as to be indifferent in the return of a mayor's posse. But a particularly questioning group was already waiting for Forge as he reined in by the sheriff's office.

'Leo.' A mule-faced man kneed his big white mule forward. 'The council meets tonight as usual. You won't be callin' it off, will you?'

'No, it'll be seven o'clock . . . *as usual*,' Forge promised, calling the man something unflattering under his breath.

'You catch them bandidos, Mayor? You give 'em a little throat trouble?' another one asked.

Taking no notice, Forge waved aside a path for himself and Jack as they stepped across the walkway to the door.

'Did you get the money back, or did they escape with that too?' another voice joined in sarcastically.

'Yeah, there's some here who lost just about everything to that scum,' the mule-face grumbled.

'Who's that with you, Mayor Forge? Is he one of 'em?' a youngster wanted to know.

Forge reached the door and opened it; before entering, turned to face those who were pressing close. 'They got away . . . outran us. They had mounts for the work, clear-foots, most of 'em. Undertaker's got three bodies you can feast your eager eyes on before he buries 'em.'

'Who are they?' the boy continued his questions.

'Two of 'em belonged to the bunch who robbed

the bank. The other one was an outsider who just happened to get in the way.'

The boy had more questions, as did mule-face. But corpses brought a frisson of local excitement, and Forge took the opportunity. He motioned for Jack to step inside, and he banged the door shut behind them.

Jack couldn't think of much to contribute at the moment, thinking it best to remain silent. He cast his eyes about the room, noted the iron-bound cell doors at the rear, the desk with its rowel-scarred top, the pot-bellied stove and wood-box, the locked rifle and pistol rack on the wall behind the desk. He watched as Forge checked the stove and added fresh wood, gave the embers a poke and settled a coffee pot to warm.

'Anyone would think this was the mayor's office,' he said quietly. 'You look real homey.'

'Hah. I've spent enough time here. Sheriff sends out somewhere East for his belly-wash, so unwind an' take a can. There's plenty of houses where you can get good fixin's, later on.'

Jack was barely aware of Forge's praise for the quality of the sheriff's coffee. His attention had already moved to Reb Fawcett. With the man dead, it was as though the last page of a book had been torn out. It was over, and it hadn't ended the way he'd avowed it must. Where could he go from here? Over time, the men who'd framed him were likely scattered to as many far away places. Realistically, how was he going to seek out and find any one of them now? What's more, did he still have the tenacity, was the fuse still lit?

'I can only guess at how an' what you must be thinking, Jack,' Forge interrupted his thoughts. 'But for what it's worth, I reckon you should forget justice, or how you'd got it planned. Right now is how it is. Spend time on what you can make a difference to. Not what you can't.'

A man limped in from the rear, carrying an armful of wood. He was an older man with rat-tailed hair and favoured one leg. He dropped kindling into the box, squinted briefly at Jack then nodded a greeting at Forge. 'Doc says the sheriff's gonna live.' He wiped his palms across the front of his tight, pea coat. 'They're buryin' our two boys tomorrow. I hope there's help for the diggin'.'

Forge nodded solemnly, poked at the embers again. 'Jack, Charlie Wei's just walked in,' he said without looking up. 'I know 'cause I can smell him. He's the stove up ol' heathen who takes care of things around here. Charlie Wei, meet Jack Calveron.'

Wei nodded. 'How do. I'm stove up all right, an' fed up. Just about everythin', except sopped an' cleaned up.'

'I was told not to eat soap and wash with it,' Jack said and extended his hand.

The old Chinaman took a bow of greeting. He had a glint in his eye, was grinning from ear to ear. He appraised Jack, from the pale blue eyes to the dusted toes of the boots, the grime of travel, the walnut grip of the big Colt. 'You're not a goddamn physic pedlar then,' he stated.

Jack smiled. 'No, I'm not one of those.'

'Jack's agreed to swear-in as our new deputy. For how long's up to him,' Forge said to satisfy some of Charlie Wei's Oriental inquisitiveness.

'Or until some feller back-shoots him.' Wei's dark eyes glimmered, met Jack's and held for a long moment. 'This is a bad town, mister, an' it's gettin' more bad every goddamn minute. We get all kinds of rubbish blown in. Huh, you think *I* got a whiff? Wait till you pin on that star, then you'll see.'

'You're talkin' through that coolie hat of yours, Charlie.' Forge chided the old man mildly and with a grin. 'It ain't as bad, as all that. Some days there's no more'n a lost dog. Las Cruces is no worse than any other town along the Rio Grande.'

'That so?' Wei sniffed disdainfully. 'One hour ago, two fellers shot each other dead right outside o' this office. While they was layin' there, there was more fightin' with guns over at the Paraiso. An' some bull-whacker drove in claimin' his family was set upon an' robbed beside Catwalk Bridge. We all know who's responsible for *that.*'

Before Forge could venture a reply, Wei was talking to Jack. 'I hope you know how to use that goddamn hog-leg you're wearin'. You're goin' to need it if you stay too long in this town.'

Without waiting for any kind of response from Forge or Jack, Charlie Wei shrugged and turned away. He went out the way he'd come in, dragging his stiff leg and leaving the back, side-door ajar.

Jack watched him go, then took a chair and accepted the cup of hot coffee.

'Charlie's some kind o' character,' Forge explained. 'A whole crew o' Chinese emigrants were out on the flood plain. They were making for California, but somehow Charlie got himself separated an' ended up here. But he's sharper than he looks, or how he likes to sound. He went partner shares in a small silver claim.'

'So how'd he end up carrying firewood?' Jack asked casually.

'Because he didn't think to bang in a few props. He got caught when part of the roof collapsed . . . wasn't much use from then on. His partner made him an offer and bought him out. The sheriff gives him work doing a few light chores around the place, makes both of 'em feel more worthwhile.'

Forge frowned, hesitated before he went on, 'Charlie reckons it was a sting, reckons his partner was fronting for Erskine Weaver. They were doing all right, but, by the time they split the profits, there wasn't much left over. There never was going to be, according to Charlie, so he wasn't too troubled with having to sell his share of the diggings. But then, and almost immediately, they struck a seam and it sort of stuck in his craw . . . if Chinamen have such a thing. The partner's long gone, but Weaver isn't. Charlie believes he was tricked, that Weaver was behind the set-up.'

Jack sipped the coffee, raised an eyebrow because

41

it was as good as Forge had suggested. 'It's been done before and will be again,' he said. 'Who's Erskine Weaver?'

'In these parts, they call his type, augur ... big augur,' Forge said. 'His mine's prospering, an' he throws his weight around a bit. He's got himself a tough crew, and when they hit town on a Friday night, there's not much that's safe.'

'Charlie reckons it should be him riding the cat wagon, does he?'

'Well, no, Jack, there's the thing: Charlie reckons the mine can't be doing as well as it appears. And *he* should know.'

'So what else does this interesting old Chinaman reckon?'

'That Weaver's proceeds are coming from robberies, rather than dug from a dry mine.'

'Is there a chance he's right?'

'Yeah, why not? I already said, Charlie Wei never reckoned on the mine making his fortune. As far as Weaver's concerned, it wouldn't be the first time someone set up a decoy at home for what they're doing away.'

Jack nodded perceptively. 'Yeah, tell me about it.'

'The sheriff's been looking into it, but I don't think he's come up with much so far,' Forge continued. Then he downed his own coffee, while rummaging in the top drawer of the office desk. 'Yeah, here it is. The badge ... your badge,' he said. 'You'll get voted in at the meeting tonight. From then on, it'll be official. Now I guess we'd better go see the doc, see how the poor feller's doing.'

Not totally stirred or enthused, Jack got to his feet, thought he was probably showing signs of weariness.

But it was Forge who got in first. 'I don't know about you Jack, but I'd like to be headed for my sack . . . any sack . . . literally,' he said.

They left their mounts hitched to the rail outside, crossed the street and walked the boards to Dr McKrew's surgery. McKrew, a tall, thin, hairless man welcomed Leo Forge with a brief familiarity, silently waved both men inside before quickly closing the door.

'Something worrying you, Mac?' Forge enquired.

'Sure there's something worrying me,' McKrew snapped back irritably. 'This town's going down the john, that's what's worrying me. What with bank robberies and killings, shoot-outs and wild brawling. It's getting so bad, Leo, decent folk will clear this town. They'll think where they came from's not so bad after all.'

Forge coughed and cleared his throat. 'How's our sheriff?' he replied evasively.

'He's been in here for worse. It's not *him* I'm concerned about.'

'If it's the way of life, Doc, remember old pills don't get rich on peace an' quiet.' Forge walked past him impatiently, pushed open a door and walked into an adjoining room.

Jack felt as though he should introduce himself but he didn't, nodded politely as he followed Forge.

A man was sitting sideways on to them. He had a hand clasped over each knee and his legs were bent over the edge of a surgery camp-bed. His chest was tightly bandaged and he looked up as they entered, grinned ruefully at Forge.

'Hello, Lewis,' Forge said. 'The doc says he's not concerned about you, you're going to be OK. I've brought someone I want you to meet. Jack Calveron, and he's going to be your new deputy.'

Jack stepped forward and pushed his hand out. The sheriff raised his own hand in response, and the men's eyes met in greeting. Recognition came at the same moment, and the years immediately fell away. They weren't in a doctor's surgery, 100 miles from the New Mexico border, then. They were standing in a courtroom back in Tucson, Arizona; a crowded room that had been listening to evidence against the US Marshal Jackson Calveron.

Iciness crept into Jack's marrow, his pale-blue eyes taking on a glittering chill. With Reb Fawcett's death, the others scattered to where he'd unlikely ever find them, it had looked like the end of his quest. But now Lewis Berry's hand had gripped his in welcome, was already slipping away as the recognition dawned.

'Calveron. Marshal Calveron,' Berry rasped.

'You two know each other?' Forge glanced curiously from one to the other. 'An' there's me thinking Las Cruces was beyond the reach of happenstance.'

'It *is*. This is meant to be.' There was a shadow of contempt in Jack's tone. Not only had he caught up with one of the men who had lied to ruin him, but the man was an elected officer of the law. Berry was the sheriff of Las Cruces, and Jack was just about to swear allegiance to him.

Jack looked into the face that was now pasty from loss of blood. He saw that five years hadn't altered it much, although the man carried a few wrinkles around the eyes and pock marks in the cheeks. But the face had been clearly implanted in Jack's mind when he'd been confronted with a prosecution of astonishing lies and a duplicitous jury.

'It's been a long time,' Jack said. 'I'd say five years almost to the day.'

'In that case there's likely been a few changes,' Forge said, and turned to leave. 'I'll leave you to talk 'em over.' He paused a moment and grinned back at Berry. 'There's a council meeting tonight, Lewis, if you feel up to it. Perhaps your deputy can lend an arm.'

'Yeah, I'll make it . . . *we'll* make it.' Berry watched Forge go, then, under Jack's withering stare, he lapsed into a long moment of silence. 'Thanks,' he said finally. 'Thanks for not saying too much . . . anything.'

'Don't thank me. You're coming back to Tucson.'

Berry winced as he tried to raise himself from the camp-bed. He shook his head. 'I've changed, Calveron. I'm not the man you knew. I'm the sheriff of Las Cruces.'

'Yeah. Like the mayor says, there's likely been a few changes. But I'm not one of 'em, Berry. You tried to have me hanged, you son-of-a-bitch. Five years of

45

my life sewing mail bags and breaking rocks, while you climbed the ladder of achievement.'

Berry took a few shallow breaths. 'I know. An' in that time I've go to be respected an' looked up to. So I won't be goin' back to Tucson now. Not after all this time.'

'You don't have a choice. You're going to find out what it's like to have your life busted apart.'

'I can understand your crave for retribution, Calveron, an' I won't make excuses for what we did. You stood in the way, that's all. It weren't personal.'

'That's all?' Jack grated angrily. 'You put a mark on my name, trashed my life, an' it wasn't *personal?*' You're going back to wipe the slate clean. *Then* I'll think about whether you've got prospects.'

Jack stood back, purpose coursing through him once again. He looked around the room, snatched a bloodied shirt from the washstand and tossed it to Berry. 'We're going. Get dressed,' he said.

6

With the approach of full dark, Fausto Salt rode calmly through the rail yard and stock corrals at the western end of Las Cruces. He had Wallace Trench and Gethin Pintura alongside him, although Pintura's appearance had been altered considerably by a clean-shaven chin and closely cropped hair. Such was the effect of Pintura's fresh look, that in poor light he could pass for a youth of fifteen or sixteen. His face was more open, almost devoid of its truer, more evil nature, although Salt and Trench still thought twice before an exchange of significant mockery.

To help the impression, Pintura was without his long-barrelled Colt. He was wearing a clean, hickory shirt and trousers, and the toes of his boots almost supported a gleam.

'It's a fact that only honest folk have shiny boots,' Salt had said. 'But now you're a greener, an' ready for the stringin'. Huh, 'cept it's *them* who's gettin' strung. Just you remember that, when you charm those guards.'

Pintura gave out uneasy noises. He felt vulnerable without his Colt, unhappy about the loss of his long hair. 'Hell, Fausto, the last time I had this done, one o' them hurdy-gurdy girls in Albuquerque said it was like eatin' chilli without chillies,' he complained. His cheeks tingled sorely from the shave that Salt had insisted on, and the clothes irritated his skin. He had unbridled faith in Salt and his doings, but it was wavering slightly.

They rode further into town and hitched their mounts to a rail alongside the boardwalk of the Prosperity Hotel. Salt went straight up to the desk and booked two rooms. 'One double for me an' my partner, an' a single for the kid,' he told the clerk.

The clerk spared them only a brief glance, pushing the register in front of them and turning back for the keys. Salt made the advance payment, then went upstairs, saw that their rooms had the advantage of being adjoined.

'Yeah, this'll do us fine,' he said to Trench. 'Now, go look for a livery. Get the horses stabled, an' meet me back here as soon as you can. Geth, you can take your little walk to the depository. Gawp at everythin' you see, as if you've never seen spit before. An' that means stayin' well away from whiskey an' women,' he warned. 'If anyone speaks to you, be polite. Especially if they ask what you learned at school today.'

Salt and Trench sniggered for a short moment, then Salt's face hardened. 'I can only imagine what this is doin' to you, Geth, but if it works, the rest of our lives might not be quite so miserable,' he declared, adding a small encouraging smile.

Pintura began to protest again, but changed his mind, again. Salt hadn't completely unveiled his plan, but Pintura knew that when the time came, the man would do as he always did and confide in him completely.

The town was getting its second start to the day. Lights were being lit in the stores, at step-offs along the boardwalks, corners of alleyways and intersections. A saloon ahead of him blazed with lantern light that, together with the sounds of profanities and pianolas, spilled from open windows and double swing doors. An assortment of wagons continued to roll along the streets, horses and mules bringing in their riders for the town's night revelry in and off the main street.

Pintura walked by the striking, tall columns that fronted the Las Cruces Depository. The building was closed now, and had two guards posted outside. 'An' I bet there's one or two *inside*,' he muttered to himself. 'An' maybe others *outside* coverin' a break-in, or a getaway. *Maybe right now.*'

He slowed his walk, gawping open-mouthed at the gold-painted eagle right above the bank's doorway. His cheeks were smooth and shiny in the light from a corner lamp, and he was aware that both guards were now watching him. He pretended not to notice, letting his gaze wander around. He was trying to look as though everything he was seeing was magical and new, not just interesting features of the bank building.

He turned slowly as one of the guards moved near to him. 'What are you guardin' in there?' he asked, meeting the man's gaze with a friendly grin. 'Must be real valuable.'

'You got business here?' the guard asked sternly.

'Me, no. I'm just lookin'. I never seen a place so big.' Pintura retained his grin, while the guard ran a watchful eye over him.

'Where are you from, kid?' he wanted to know.

'Place don't have a name. There's nothin' there except our cabin. It's near the Shosh Hole, but Pa says most folk's never heard o' that, either.'

'Yeah?' the guard replied with a scratch of his head. He was off duty soon, and such a conversation made him feel curiously worthwhile, less bored. 'So what you doin' in town?'

'Pa's business. He says I'm to mind my own. Just look around an' keep out o' trouble.'

'Seems to me a bit unfair. You seen dancin' girls before?' the guard enquired with a knowing wink towards his partner.

'Lawks, mister. I ain't ever seen a *town* before.'

'Well, you keep away from anywhere that's got noise comin' from it. Someone's likely to come out an' shoot you for just passin' by.'

'I don't have a gun . . . not one to carry on my belt, anyhow. Pa says the only gun I'm havin' is the ol' squirreler for shootin' pot critters.'

'This pa o' yours sounds like real straight goods.

Where is he, kid?'

'In the Prosperity Hotel.'

'Well, look here. I've got me a night duty, guardin' supplies for the mines. So, if you're still knockin' around in fifteen minutes, I'm walkin' down to the rail yard. I've got an hour to kill, so I could show you some o' the town. On the way back, if you ain't been shot already, you can poke your head round the door of one of our friendlier dog holes.'

Pintura considered for a moment, tried another smile. 'Probably not. Sounds too close to trouble.'

'Why not go check with your pa?'

'Nah. He won't mind me just lookin'. Besides, he said I wasn't to bother him.' Pintura gave the guard his broadest and best smile. The clincher, he thought.

With the palm of his hand covering the grip of his holstered Colt, Jack Calveron ushered Lewis Berry out of the recovery room and into the front office of the surgery. Doctor McKrew saw immediately what was happening, although he obviously didn't understand it. He backed, off stood bemused as Jack motioned for Berry to open the door to the street.

'Where are you going?' McKrew's voice was raised to a higher pitch, and unsteady. 'The man's a patient and still under my care. What's happening?' he demanded.

'He's decided to unburden you,' Jack said. 'Inform the interested parties.'

'Inform? Inform them with *what*?'

'That we're headed out of town. Him an' me both. We're heading west, an' could be gone for some time.'

'But he's the *sheriff*,' McKrew spluttered. 'Sheriffs can't just leave. What happens to the town? He's our law and order . . . has been for four, five years. Who *are* you, mister? The mayor never said.'

'Jackson Calveron. And you've lost a sheriff *an'* his deputy elect.'

'What are we supposed to do without any law?'

'Elect someone new, before you slip further down that john.'

Jack opened the door and nodded for Berry to step outside. They walked the boards a bit, then crossed the street with more than one questioning stare following them. But Berry kept his mouth shut, his lips still drawn and bloodless, his gaze set directly ahead.

'You know what's so useful here, Berry?' Jack said calmly. 'It's you not being able to say a word. What would you tell 'em, eh? Not the truth, an' you can't lie because I'm right beside you. All the same, until I say otherwise, keep real quiet.'

When the two men reached the jailhouse, Berry opened the door and went inside. He walked up to the desk, turning about slowly, looking at the trappings of office, *his* office. Then an anger started to beat inside him. He was unarmed and hurt, but he was considering his chances. He saw the rest of his life as a lot to lose.

As if to shadow his thoughts, Charlie Wei emerged from the gloom of the cells. He flicked a match to the wick of an oil lamp, turned the flame high. Dusk had crept deep into the room, and only when the old Chinaman's eyes became accustomed to the lamp's glare, did he see the look on Berry's face, the set of Jack's stance in the doorway.

Before Wei had a chance to say anything, Jack stepped forward, towering over him. 'Saddle a horse, Charlie. Pack a couple of bags with what you think the sheriff might need for a long ride. Don't take too long over it, either.'

The old man darted a worried look at Berry.

'Just do as he says, Charlie,' Berry said evenly. 'He won't listen to any argument, an' it would take too long to explain.'

'Yeah, like five years,' Jack muttered. He drew his Colt, pointed it at Charlie. 'Go on, get goin'. An' don't try any Chinee tricks,' he warned.

Wei withdrew slightly until a snarl curled his thin mouth. He had a stove-up leg, and a lot of years weighed on him. Because of that, he didn't scare too easily, wasn't about to leave without some sort of resistance. With a throaty murmur, and in defiance of the big Colt, he limped a couple of steps forward. Then he let his hips drop, and swiped the edge of his right hand in a high fast arc at Jack's wrist.

But Jack had anticipated something of the sort, and his Colt twisted in his grip. His hand moved very quickly, blocking the blow aimed at him.

Charlie Wei sucked in air, gasping at the sharp,

sudden pain.

'How the hell are you going to load those saddle-bags with busted fingers?' Jack rasped. 'I thought you people were meant to be clever.' With one hand, Jack gripped the front of the old man's pea coat and pulled him close. 'Any more trouble, an' I'll blow a hole in your sheriff so big, it'll take a whole Chinaman's head to plug the bleeding. You understand, Charlie? Get to work. An' saddle a goddamn horse.'

Wei edged away. There was still a trace of threat in his inscrutable eyes, but he made no second attempt to fight. He looked from Jack to Berry, back to Jack. He didn't know what it was all about, but seemed to accept it was bad trouble, that there was very little he could do about it. 'I'll go,' he said, and moved away, leaving the door ajar as he limped off towards the livery.

7

Darkness had settled across Las Cruces. Along the street, lamps had been lit and the heavy roil of daytime dirt and dust had settled. Jack ushered Lewis Berry out of the sheriff's office and into the saddle.

Charlie Wei stood helpless, upset at the fact that he hadn't made another attempt to prevent the men leaving. Still with no notion about what was going on, he watched as Calveron and Berry pulled away from the hitch rail, picking up the unhurried flow of traffic on the street. Then with a muttered curse, and a spit in the dust, he went as fast as he could to seek out Leo Forge.

'Just keep riding,' Jack told Berry. 'Don't look back, just head for the end of town.'

'How much further than that do you think we'll get?' Berry said. 'They'll have a posse after us before we've gone a mile.'

'Yeah, I've seen the makings of that crew. I'm not too fussed about being able to dodge 'em.'

Jack saw a few curious faces turned their way as

they approached the settlements at the end of town, but none was openly hostile or worth worrying about. Doctor McKrew hadn't yet found time to rouse the town, or had thought better of it. Charlie Wei would have made it to the mayor's house, so it wouldn't be long before there were guns out hunting for him, albeit unskilled and very small bore.

'All the same, we'll put in some miles before first light,' Jack continued coolly. 'If it's Forge, and he assembles the same outfit, it shouldn't be difficult to give 'em the slip.'

Berry said nothing. He was looking out at the dark shapes of the low-built houses beyond the traders' cabins and supply tents. He'd settled in Las Cruces to build a fresh life for himself, attemped to gain respect, to make a success. He felt that up to a point he had done, carrying out his duties as town sheriff. But now that was over, and that was the rub; he'd always known that someday it would end. He'd built a new life on shifting sand.

'How'd you find me?' he asked quietly. 'How'd you come to Las Cruces in the first place.'

'It wasn't the first place. I was trailing Reb Fawcett.' Jack shifted slightly in the saddle, took a sidelong glance at Berry's pasty face, before he continued. 'I got out of the stockade an' learned of Fawcett being alive. He was hiding out near the border . . . Nogales. I went after him and he ran. Ran a few long goddamn miles before he finally headed this way.'

'So you've caught up with him?'

'Yes an' no. He was shot dead by the bunch who robbed your bank. I figured that was the end of the trail. I had no leads an' nowhere else to turn. I wouldn't have agreed to take the job Forge offered me if there'd been any kind of trail to follow.'

Berry nodded, went silent again. So it had been a quirk of fate, a chance in a million, he was thinking. Fate, the one thing you can't escape from. He bowed his head and closed his eyes, allowing the horse to walk alongside Jack's claybank mare. In the out-of-town stillness, he caught the odour of fried meat, the town's night murmurings, a man's rowdiness piercing the dark. With his eyes shut, the town was implanting itself on his mind. Las Cruces, where he'd come to settle and forget.

It had been a clever scheme and not entirely Berry's. There'd been six of them who'd conspired to be rid of Jackson Calveron. Ten of them who wanted the US marshal out of the way while they continued with their wrong-doing. They had fully intended to see Jack hanged, and though it hadn't worked out that way, it did get him banged up in Redrock Stockade for five years. That was time enough to fatten their pockets, put Tucson well behind them, before Jack earned his release.

Five years and Berry had put the whole incident behind him. He'd settled in Las Cruces, worked for and accepted the job as sheriff, even nailed up the wood-carved inscription that read: *A broken sack don't hold corn.* Reckon I know what it means, now, he thought bitterly.

They were just beyond the outskirts of town, and still there was no sign of any pursuit. Jack glanced back, then peered forward into the darkness. He saw some lights not far to their left, and he heard Berry mutter something, watched him check his mount and turn towards him.

'If I promise not to give you any trouble, to ride all the way back to Tucson, an' not try an' escape, will you grant me one favour?' the man asked quietly.

Jack stared at him. 'At this moment, *favours* are way outside o' my gift, Berry. What the hell are you going on about?'

'I want to see my stepdaughter.' Berry's request was simple but larded with feeling. 'My wife had a girl by a previous marriage. She died after a year with me, and I kind o' took the kid as my own. That's the way it still is. Her name's Raphaela.'

Jack grunted at the surprise disclosure. 'You should have said, goddamnit. Now, you're telling me you want to say goodbye, that she lives across there?'

'Yeah, one o' the old green timber houses. It'll only take a minute, an' she doesn't have to know where we're going, or why.'

'Can't say I understand the sentiment, Berry. I never had the chance. But knowing she's not your blood kin, might make a difference if you try an' gull me,' Jack warned. 'Say your piece an' we ride on.'

The small house was a neatly proportioned four-roomed affair. It was set well back from the road, partly screened by a stand of smoke-thorn, and a wedge of yellow light fell from one of two front windows. As the two men reined to a halt and Berry dismounted, the door opened and the slim figure of a girl stood framed against the glare.

Jack cursed under his breath as the girl called a greeting for Berry.

'Pa,' she said, stepping forward hesitantly. 'Are you all right? I was getting worried. Leo Forge told me you'd been shot, but it wasn't serious. Said it was best for me to wait here.'

'Hello, Ella.' Berry cleared his throat, glanced at Jack and then at the girl. 'I'm OK, but I've got to leave town. I've got business out in Tucson that has to be settled.'

Jack swore again, silently, wondered why Berry had to get himself a family, even a make-believe one. The girl's eyes were already on him, wondering who he was without asking. She was young, he guessed about seventeen or eighteen. Her hair was long, probably let down at the end of the day, and she wore a plain homespun dress and ankle boots.

Berry took a step forward and grasped the girl's hands in his. 'I'm sorry, Ella. I gave my word.'

'Gave your word to who? Him? About what? I'm coming with you. I can pack a few things. No more or less than what you're obviously travelling with.'

'I have to go alone.'

'Why?' Again the girl stared up at Jack, longer this time. A gut feeling told her that Berry was leaving against his wish, that he was calling by to say that she wouldn't be seeing him for a while, probably a long while. Her stepfather would have introduced an old friend or an official acquaintance, and a sudden rush of resentment towards Jack gripped her. She edged sideways away from the door, positioned herself between the two men, shielding Berry from the unmistakable big Colt on Jack's hip. She tensed herself, clenched her fists as though ready for a fight.

'You're leaving because of this man here,' she challenged, keeping her eyes on Jack but speaking to Berry. 'He's forcing you to ride off, I know it. Who is he, Pa? What are you doing with him?'

'Please, Ella,' Berry attempted to calm her. 'Please don't make something out of it. It's a kind of business trip, an' I'll be back. I promise.' At that, Berry expected Jack to say something, something contrary, but he didn't.

Jack cleared his throat. 'We're wasting time,' he said and nodded at Berry.

'Take care, girl.' Berry gave Raphaela an affectionate hug and swung back into the saddle.

Raphaela shook her head sadly and reached out. She made one quick wave, then dropped both hands to her sides to disguise any give-away feeling, stepping back as the two men turned their mounts away. Although her feelings were for her stepfather, her steely, hate-filled gaze never left Jack.

8

A short moment before the rider appeared from the deep shadow at the side of the house, Jack's mare snorted with unease.

'That's far enough, Jack. Hold up,' Leo Forge called out. Immediately, a second rider emerged from the shelter of a poled lean-to. Then a third and a fourth man rose up from the smoke-thorn. All of them were armed.

Jack cursed, made a half-hearted move for his Colt, even as one of the voices yelled for him not to.

'Best not to make a move, Jack. One or two o' these fellers are still lookin' for compensation.' Leo Forge's words cut the air decisively. 'I guessed what had happened back there in McKrew's office. I held off waiting to see what you'd do about it.'

'Well now you know, and we meet again.' Jack moved his hands slowly, clasped them across the saddle horn as Forge and his men closed in.

'Yeah, an' it's your mistake,' Forge said flatly. 'How the hell did you figure on making it back to Tucson,

61

even if you'd kept on going? Did you think the town would let you get away with it? You're kidnappin' its sheriff, goddamnit.'

Forge had a Colt in his fist and he prodded it at Jack in anger as he continued. 'I offered you a job as deputy to Berry here, an' you took it into that crazy block of yours to run off with him to Arizona. Well, as of now, that offer's retracted Jack, and I'm telling you to ride on. If you come back, you'll be shot from the saddle.'

'As long as you don't set more than half-a-dozen o' your mutton-punchin' posse on me. In the past, I've had trouble going up against that number.'

'For God's sake, stop it there, both o' you.' Lewis Berry kneed his horse forward, driving hard into the shoulder of Forge's sturdy chestnut mount. 'I had it coming, Leo,' he rasped. 'I did more than break the law. I wronged him bad an' he went to jail for it. I lied to be rid of him. Now I have to pay.'

'He's got no authority, no jurisdiction here. An' he's not a lawman any more.' Forge shook his head. 'He can't take you back. You're the sheriff of Las Cruces, New Mexico, an' there's not a goddamn thing he can do about *that.*'

'Maybe so, Leo. But he's dead set on havin' a try. By going with him, I'm saving us all a lot of time an' trouble.'

The silence that followed was heavily charged, Jack's unwavering stare locked with Forge's. They faced each other while the men and the girl steadily crowded closer.

'Leo, listen to me a moment.' Berry spoke quietly, but hoping his words would push the mayor into lowering the barrel of his Colt. 'You don't know the truth of it. In a way, I welcome what's come about. It means I don't have to spend any more o' my life wondering *when*, not *if*. Besides, I gave my word. I promised that if he let me say goodbye to my daughter . . . stepdaughter, I'd go peaceably. It's too late now to do otherwise.'

'It's too late if you go with him, Lew. We've rode out here to take you back, not wish you bon voyage.'

'I'm goin', Leo. That's it.'

'OK, we're not here to help you. It's the town I'm worried about. How about that?'

Berry smiled grimly, shook his head in resignation. He was going back to Tucson, facing the consequences of a crime he'd tried so hard to escape from. He'd known it from the moment Jack Calveron walked into the doctor's surgery in Las Cruces.

Realizing his new tack was useless, and unmindful of the girl's presence, Forge cursed strongly. He looked at the men reining in close, glanced once more at Berry, then shrugged and holstered his Colt. 'How many more times do I lose today?' he seethed, waving the others to withdraw.

Jack calmed slightly as the riders fell back. But knowing that any one of Forge's misguided gunhands might retaliate, he remained very alert. He was almost at the end of his mission, wanted no more slip-ups. He had one of the men who could disclose the miscarriage of justice. He could ride 250 miles to look Tucson in the eye, watch some of the local folk squirm at the thought of what they had chosen to believe, what the jury had convicted him of. For the thousandth time, he would sit in the small court-room and listen to the lies, the ruthless scheme that six men had perpetrated. Only the *next* time, it wouldn't be a hopeless dream. A righteous upholder and administrator of the law would be confessing the perjury.

'You're not fit to ride, Lew. Doc said you lost a lot o' blood, an' that wound'll need a clean dressing.' The strain was clear in Forge's voice as he turned from Berry to Jack. 'For God's sake, he'll never make it. He'll be dead before you get to the border, let alone the middle of Arizona.'

'Then we're both taking a chance. I'll take mine, same as him. Good try, Forge. I can see how you got to be mayor.'

'I'll make it.' Berry sat straighter in the saddle, nodded to Jack. 'If you've had enough o' this jawbone, let's head out. They'll leave us be.'

Jack dragged on the reins and hauled the mare around, holding up while Berry went ahead. The man had given his word there'd be no trouble, but it was Leo Forge whom Jack was still worried about. No one gets to be mayor without an occasional decep-tion. Jack was in no frame of mind for chances, and he was feeling the weary pinch of trail's end.

As Berry turned his horse to the westward trail, there came the sudden rattle of shots from some-where near the centre of town. Everyone turned to look, and within moments a rider came riding wildly through the darkness towards them.

'Hell, Forge, you're right about this place,' Jack yelled out. 'Sounds like it can't hold anything in.'

Guns were now banging along the main street, together with boisterous hollering and women screaming.

Suddenly, fearful of a repetition of Reb Fawcett's death, Jack cursed and heeled the claybank to Berry's side. 'Get back. Take cover by the house,' he commanded.

The rider came on. He was crouching low in the saddle, his spurs raking the horse's flanks, urging for greater speed.

'Goddamnit, he is coming for us,' Jack shouted, as he saw the rider's head came up, together with a fistful of big revolver.

Jack yelled again for Berry to get out of his way. He reached out and grabbed the reins of Berry's mount, pulling the claybank around as he did so. Before he had time to draw his own Colt, he saw the orange spurt of the rider's gun flash against the night. He heard the crash of the shot, then, as the light smacked against his eyes, he was plucked from the saddle and hammered into blackness, cursed into oblivion.

9

Gethin Pintura played his part with the assurance of a professional. He was the young greener, still wet behind the ears, but with it went friendliness, an innocence of everyday life, many of its facts. He strolled the lamp-lit main street, the off-duty bank guard pointing out the places he thought might be of interest. He gazed around him with a natural looking curiosity at the least impressive buildings, then exhibited bewilderment at the crowded windows of a double-fronted mercantile. He smiled in mock disbelief when told there was so much in store, it needed two floors to stock and display it.

'I never knew there were such places,' he exclaimed. 'I just never seen anythin' like all this. Ever.'

'Not enough years for your majority, an' too many for a sumac an' horehound, eh, kid? But not for a taste o' the counter canary who parcels up the dry goods, I'll wager,' the guard said, with a boorish chortle.

Pintura gave a look of not fully understanding, before pointing towards the Depository. 'The place where you work; what's the big eagle for?' he asked.

'A show of strength ... confidence. It's an American eagle.'

'Hmm. What do they sell, then?'

'They don't really sell, not like a regular store,' the guard started to explain. 'It's specially built for keeping all the town's money. All the folks' hard-earned dollars.'

'Pheeew. Pa keeps his in baccy tins out by Jones's place,' Pintura said.

'I don't reckon we'd get all the town's loot into them,' the guard replied. 'Tell you what, if you're still around this time tomorrow, I'll show you inside. It'll be quiet then. Have you had anything to eat recently?'

'No, I guess not. Not recently.'

'Nor have I. We'll have somethin' in here. Get somethin' that puts meat on your bones. Ha, you look more like a desert grasshopper.' The guard carried the employment stamp of brawn over brain. Minty Book was a railroad jackleg from way back. An ox of a man whose air of sincerity hid the lack of common sense.

After they had eaten their beef, biscuits and gravy, Pintura made a show of fumbling awkwardly in his trouser pockets. But Book was the trusting dupe; he drew some coins from a hide purse and insisted on paying for both of them.

'Yow. Mr Tippybob,' Pintura exclaimed. 'Where'd

you get all that? You take it from where you get to guard?'

'No. I earned it from there. Anyways it ain't much more'n pennies. Let's go see if there's anythin' happenin' round back of the Paraiso. You'd like that, an' I start at the yard shortly.'

They stepped from the heat of the grub house, back into the cooler street, stood watching as a group of men swung their horses away from the Take A Chance Hotel.

Book pulled back slightly, took Pintura's arm as the riders swept by. 'They're Erskine Weaver's boys,' he said. 'Mean sons o' bitches, every one of 'em. Make sure you keep well out o' their way.'

Breathlessly, Pintura watched the riders. He said nothing, making a mental note to find out more about them. But it would sound like happy-go-lucky interest, brought on by being callow. Remembering what Fausto Salt had said about plenty of hooters being eager to throw in with them, he thought there might be something to the Weaver boys, then immediately wondered if they could be after the same thing. He saw them haul in their mounts outside the Paraiso saloon, turning away as they stamped across the boardwalk, arms eagerly stretched to the batwings.

'You see where they went?' he said eagerly. 'Do you reckon they've gone to see them dancin' girls? Let's go take a look. We don't have to go inside . . . just sort o' walk on by.'

'I dunno, kid. Lookin' can bring you bad luck with

68

them fellers.' Book scratched his chin, frowning. 'Like I said, they're real mean. An' they know the sheriff ain't too lively after the robbery. They'll be causin' trouble tonight. You can count the minutes. Perhaps we should move on.'

Pintura shrugged as though it didn't matter. 'Yeah, OK. Trouble's what Pa said I had to stay away from. Let's go back this way.'

They had only walked twenty yards in the other direction, when someone stepped from the shadows ahead. As they drew level, Pintura glimpsed an open doorway, a lamp, glowing softly behind a red shade. The girl's glossy mouth smiled warmly at them, the rose cologne screamed a temptation and Book uttered an admiring grunt. The girl set her head a little to one side, catching the dark eyes of Pintura, she gave an unmistakable nod towards the door.

Book's big hand wrapped around Pintura's arm, tugged to drag him away. 'There's some things you've got to learn, kid. One of 'em's to stay away from this sort of doorway until you've done some ripenin'.'

Pintura bridled. He started to protest, for the moment forgetting the role he was supposed to be playing. The girl stood there swaying slightly, tempting him, as Book tried to lead him away. He wrenched himself free, the copperhead black eyes unexpectedly flashing fire.

'Get your maws off me, you great barrel o' lard. You don't tell me what to do. No one does.'

'But—' Book was shocked by the sudden switch of

character and he blustered. He felt the power of Pintura's venom, and a shiver ran through him.

Pintura took a few shallow breaths, struggling to compose himself. He'd made a big error and knew it. He had to act as he'd been told, else ruin all Fausto Salt's planning.

'Ah, I'm sorry. I didn't mean that,' he gulped out quickly. 'Pa told me that one day my ol' bean would make trouble.'

'Yeah, your pa knew it. Right now it's for pissin' with . . . remember that, kid. You ever pointed it at one o' them Shosh girls, or wherever it is you come from?'

'No, sir, I haven't. An' I sure am sorry.'

'OK, let's forget it. But I sure wouldn't want to be around when somethin' really upsets you,' Book accepted. 'Come on, we got to move. Me especially.'

They headed away from where the Weaver boys had hitched their mounts, and a small brooding smile worked its way across Pintura's mouth. The next day, Book had promised to show him inside the Las Cruces Depository. And Minty Book was a guard, so Gethin Pintura would be trusted, too. And Fausto Salt would be best pleased about that.

'That's where I'm headed. Over beyond those buidings.' Book pointed to a glow of light, a rising column of stack smoke. 'There's a line clear up to Mimbres an' Santa Rita, now. Folks said it would never get there, but it did. Sure is a tribute to all them railroad fellers. Used to be one myself.'

Pintura nodded absently. His attention was still

with the Paraiso, the swinging batwings and sounds within, and his throat ready for the sear of a Pass whiskey. 'Yeah, some o' that, too,' he murmured at the raucous laughter, the unmistakable noise of men and their pleasures.

'Who is this Weavil feller?' he asked Book. 'He an outlaw or somethin'? Pa said we weren't too far off o' their trail.'

Book's shoulders moved as he laughed. 'No, kid, you misunderstood him. An' it's not Weavil, it's Weaver . . . Erskine Weaver, an' he's—'

But Book had no opportunity to reply further. A man cursed, a woman screamed, and a body came crashing out through the batwings. Pintura felt the excitement, but it was in recognition of everything being in a familiar sequence.

A bullet smashed its way through the slatted doors, closely followed by one of the Weaver boys. The man looked around him, up and down the dark street. He fired again and Pintura heard the buzz, felt the pulse of a bullet passing close by.

'What the hell's the matter with you?' Pintura yelled a warning for Book to get out of the way. But the big guard was rooted to the spot and Pintura took a running dive for his legs, somewhere below the knees. As the Weaver gun blasted for a third time, the bank guard was going down like a sack of potatoes.

'Hell of watchman you make. Just gets better an' better,' Pintura gasped, as they both crashed to the boardwalk.

As Charlie Wei had warned, and Minty Book had clearly predicted, the Weaver boys were out to make trouble. They were supposed to ride into town, indulge in some fair roostering, kick up their heels. They were told not to step outside of the law, to keep near the edge, create civic unrest, enough aggravation to hold the sheriff's attention.

'Keep him worried. Goddamnit, keep everyone worried', had been Erskine Weaver's explicit instructions.

But Weaver wasn't to know that Lewis Berry would stop a bullet, and he added nothing for such an eventuality. So his word remained as it was given, his men mooching the Las Cruces streets, drifting between one drinking hole and another. They were taking on liquor at a rate that would have felled most men, provoking fights and maintaining a general feeling of nervousness. By the time they made their way to the Paraiso, they were real proddy, not one of them close to sober.

Standing at the bar, the young 'puncher looked up, tilted the battered range hat back from his forehead. Taking a sideways glance, he saw the Weaver boys – all of them were grimed with the dirt of a silver mine – carried an assortment of pistols belted high and tight around their waists. One of them was a leathery grizzler with heavy eyebrows, one corner of his mouth turned down in a continual sneer. It was a face he remembered seeing before in Las Cruces.

Only then it was set on a neck with a circle of rope around it and swinging from cross brace of Catwalk Bridge.

It was a recollection that hardened the 'puncher's jaw, tightened the corners of his eyes. Maybe there was no longer much cattle rustling across the Rio Grande's flood plain, but the brand of cow thief was burned deep.

Tom Pagham had ridden countless weary miles on his drive northwards. With the cattle sold and the men paid off, he'd packed his bedroll and turned for home, his trail bringing him through Las Cruces. He hadn't come looking for trouble; he had a young wife and child to care for. Furthermore, his wife was always telling him that, in some of the places he'd be fetching up at, life might be cheap, might take more courage to live than to die . . . that he must look out. Now, tired and thirsty he only wanted a drink or two and a bed for the night. He'd booked a room out back, above the saloon, and just about had his fill of warm beer. He would have walked out there and then if he hadn't set eyes on Goose Hollister, a man he'd presumed hanged a long time ago.

Pagham wasn't going to concern himself with how Hollister had managed to cheat the hangman. Living evidence was standing near, practically sharing a bar with him. A cow-man's loathing for rustlers stirred within him, and his right hand dropped down to his Colt. It was an older model Paterson, carried for show, doubtful protection. But he kept his hand there, waiting to see if there was a stir of recognition in Hollister's dark eyes.

A moment later, Hollister suddenly grew tense. A laugh that had been stretching his sullen mouth, fell away. He nudged the man next to him, nodded in the direction of Pagham and muttered something. The other men turned to look, and the crowd at the bar sensed the tension, prudently retreating a step or two.

The barkeep leaned forward to speak to Pagham. 'Whatever just happened, feller, leave it.' The warning came hurriedly, in a low, hoarse whisper. 'They're well liquored, an' need prey. Don't let it be you. Put your glass down an' get out.'

The crowd fell back further and an expectant murmur settled across the bar room. The Weaver boys fanned out, hands making pretend actions for their guns.

Pagham glanced to either side, saw half-a-dozen men suddenly gathered against him and then he too backed off a step. He could hear his wife's concern ringing in his ears, as he measured the distance to the door.

Hollister was grinning cruelly, the fingers of his hand curling like talons within inches of a revolver. 'Must be the chase season, boys,' he rasped. 'An' it looks like we got us a runner.'

Pagham still had his right hand near to his own Colt. His left hand rested on the bar top, close to the beer glass. 'I'm wonderin' the best way to do both those things,' he replied to the barkeep's warning, 'Like this, I guess,' he added, reacting as he spoke.

He curled his fingers around the glass, drew it sliding across the sopping counter and flung it out across the room.

A man hollered and a saloon girl screamed. The glass smashed against the wall behind Goose Hollister. He flinched, but his malicious smirk remained.

Pagham ran for the door. He hit the batwings and flung them wide, heard a roar of profanity behind him as he crashed out to the walkway. Then there was a gunshot, as he swerved to hug the shadows, a second, then a third bullet zipping closer as he stumbled forward. His only chance was to get out of town and fast. Knowing he needed cover, he leapt from the walkway, ran streetside to the mounts that were tethered outside the saloon.

As the Weaver boys came tripping and yelling through the batwings, Pagham knew his only immediate cover between them and their guns, were the mounts at the hitch rail. His own horse was stabled too far away, near the rail yard, behind the stock pens, so he was driven to a crime of which he'd never considered himself capable. 'Sorry, there's a first time for everythin',' he gasped, grabbing at the reins of the nearest buckskin. He slipped them free and, hurling himself into the saddle, dug hard with his heels.

But even before he'd reached the end of the main street, the Weaver boys were scrambling drunkenly into their saddles for their pursuit. Their curses rang out as they swung around in befuddled circles. Then they picked up on the trail of Pagham, their Colts discharging wildly into the night.

Just beyond the outskirts of town, Pagham glanced back. Against the low light of the town, he could make out the Weaver boys bearing down on him and he cursed. He raked the flanks of the stolen horse, turned back to see riders ahead, with no time to determine friend or foe, cursed louder. The riders were in his way, and he dragged out the aged Paterson. 'Go on, scare 'em off,' he rasped and jerked the trigger. He saw the men veer sharply to one side, then one of them braced himself as though in shock before collapsing from the saddle. 'Good God, I hope that wasn't me,' he huffed.

He kept on going, clasping the neck of his horse as he thundered on past, cutting north from the main trail, heading for the foothills. He heeled his spurs, while the aggrieved buckskin snorted and fought the bits. Then he turned south, took the switchback to try and confuse his pursuers.

But the Weaver boys were in no fit condition to ride, drawing to a scrappy halt as the low hogbacks loomed out of the darkness. They abandoned their chase in and around a stand of stunt pine, crossly accepting defeat.

'An' we never found out what he was starin' at you for, Goose,' one of them said.

'No, hell if I know. Perhaps he was about to stand me a drink. Let's get back an' see.'

After an hour's ride south, Tom Pagham reached Otis Flats. But he didn't go into the town. At the signpost he stopped for a while to put his thoughts together. Then he turned west towards the border, Arizona and home.

10

Jack Calveron's first conscious thought was of a crashing wave of agony behind his eyes, then a dull, ebb. But it was a kick to his brain that, for a time, recollected nothing.

Minutes later, a weak light, filtered through his closed lids, then he became aware of his head being cushioned by something soft against the back of his neck. He opened his eyes slowly and winced, blinking before closing them again.

'The bullet clipped the side of your head,' Raphaela said quietly. 'Doctor McKrew's been here. He says you'll have a concussion for a day or two. If it had hit you anywhere else, you'd more than likely be dead.'

'He said *that*?' Jack pushed at an elbow to raise himself and groaned.

'No, *I* did. He's too well mannered.'

'Huh. How about the day or two bit?' He opened his eyes again, and tried to sit up. But dizziness hit him, toppled him back to the pillow as his thoughts turned to Berry.

'My stepfather will still be here, if that's what you're worried about.' Raphaela said, the animosity clear, and as though she was aware of his thoughts. 'He gave you his word and he'll keep it.'

Jack looked up at her, saw the weariness in her eyes, the mussed hair, the lamplight making her skin look pale. Despite what she had said, the manner of it, he thought there was some concern, maybe even a care.

Raphaela gave a start of embarrassment as each of them realized that her hand was resting on his arm. She drew away, and Jack grinned, closed his eyes again as the colour crept into her cheeks. She turned away from him for a moment, took a breath then looked back.

'You've no idea the kind of man my stepfather is,' she said, now meeting his gaze coolly. 'He's told me all about the past, but it makes no difference. It's what he is now that matters to me. He's a good man, and this whole town knows it, knows him for what he is.'

Jack saw her sincerity, watching as she took a slow turn around the room before facing him again.

'He loved my mother. He knew she hadn't long to live when he married her, but it didn't spoil what they felt for each other. He told me that my mother knew all about his past, that if anything, it served to bind them closer together.'

'Yeah, well, with respect, it's a funny old way to do it. Pouring your heart out to someone who's on their deathbed. Telling them you looked a whole town in the face and lied to get an innocent man five years' hard labour. Yeah, that's what love's made of.'

'He treated me like his own. From the very beginning he was kind,' Raphaela continued unabashed.

'Yeah, *what* kind?' Jack retorted. '*He* had the chance for all of that stuff; some of us didn't.'

'Life's made up of chances, Mr Calveron. There's some you can take, and some you can't. It can be a real bitch. But I'm not letting you take him away. I won't.'

'So how do you propose to stop me?' he asked, meeting an angry tear in her eye with his own kind of unwavering stare.

'How?' She seemed surprised at the question. 'I'd be one hell of a fool to tell you that, wouldn't I? Even if I knew the answer. You're claiming he took five years—'

'I'm not *claiming*,' Jack interrupted. '*Five years* isn't something I made up.'

'Well he's given that to this town,' Raphaela persisted in her defence of Berry. 'He's not a young man, but he's worked for this town better than any man half his age would have. He's been the father I needed . . . still do. I'm not about to leave him.'

'Despite the fact he's already decided to go back to Tucson?'

Raphaela's head came up defiantly. 'You heard what Leo Forge said. You've no authority . . . certainly none in Las Cruces. If I persuade him to stay, then there's nothing you can do about it.'

'If he's the respectable member of society you say he is, a man of his word, I won't have to.'

Raphaela turned for the door, was opening it before she spoke again. 'You won't get another chance to pull a gun on him. There's enough folk in this town to see to that,' she said, leaving the room.

'I didn't pull a gun on him. He did that himself, five years ago,' Jack muttered. 'An' I'd be interested to know where the hell you did your schooling,' he added.

By the light spreading from a bedside table lamp, Jack turned his head for a look around. The room at the rear of the house was small and plainly furnished, appeared to be free from dust that would normally have blown in from across the busy town. He squinted as he looked around, guessed it had been very recently swept clean. There were patterned curtains to the window, a Navajo rug was tacked to one wall and another covered half the floor. A washstand was set with a pitcher of water, a basin and folded towel. *This must be her room, Raphaela's room,* he thought, cursing as a fist of pain hit him between the eyes. Pegs on the wall alongside the door were draped with his clothes, and he suspected they had been beaten along with the rugs. There was a small open fireplace set in the inner wall, and a clock on the mantel above said it was fifteen minutes off two o'clock. I know there's one of them in the afternoon, he thought, grimacing as he investigated his wound with his fingertips. Then he turned his head on the pillow, and closed his eyes again.

He woke to the sound of voices. The lamp was still burning, although daylight was creeping through and around the curtains. He listened to a muffled conversation and the clattering of pots that drifted from the kitchen. From the clock's new time, he guessed it was Berry and Raphaela preparing breakfast food.

He swung his legs uncertainly to the floor, tested his weight and his strength, gasping and taking deep breaths against the wave of faintness that nearly overwhelmed him. As the room wheeled around him, he sat on the edge of the bed for a few minutes. He waited until the giddiness subsided, then got to his feet, feeling his way along the wall towards his clothes.

Once dressed he drenched himself with water from the pitcher. The chill made the pain more poignant, but he felt sharper, better prepared. He looked at his Colt, but made no attempt to buckle its belt on. He dragged on his boots, took a few more puffy breaths as he bent down, then decided to go for the door.

'Calveron. What the—?' Berry was surprised, turning with a start as Jack entered the scullery.

Raphaela put down a fry pan with a small exclamation of alarm. 'The doc said you had to stay in bed for a few days. A full day at least.'

'Yeah, he's probably right,' Jack said, trying a wounded smile. 'What happened out there? Seems everyone around this town's got a shoot first policy. Haven't you got any gun laws?'

'Not if you're the Erskine Weaver boys,' Berry replied, with a slight shake of his head. 'It was some feller bein' chased from the Paraiso. Seems like they prodded him up to a gun fight, but he figured against the odds an' backed out. *Ran* out actually, takin' most o' the batwings with him. He's probably across the Mogollons by now . . . him an' one o' their horses.'

Jack sat himself down in a high-backed chair. 'Don't let me interrupt you,' he said, letting his shoulders slump tiredly.

'I was just sayin' to Raphy how the Weaver bunch have been trouble for quite a while. Ol' Erskine wants to own this town, an' judgin' the amount o' silver they appear to be haulin' from that mine of his, it'll be sooner not later.'

Jack nodded, recalling that Charlie Wei had told Leo Forge about there being a lot more to the origins of Weaver's fortune than a barren silver mine.

'It's mighty odd,' Berry went on. 'Santa Rita's where the heaviest lodes are bein' found. But he's nowhere near there, or Mimbres, *an'* it's shallow workin'. So how come he's got a whole force of men on his payroll?'

'I don't know, but I met a Chinaman who's got a view on it.'

'Yeah, Charlie Wei. You know about his beef? What he claims?' Berry asked.

'Only what Leo Forge told me. I know Wei was one of two partners, that there was an accident, and he couldn't work any more. It was Erskine Weaver who bought him out. I assumed all that was common knowledge.'

'It is,' Berry agreed. 'But probably 'cause they're makin' from it, a lot o' folk don't want to know *where* his money's comin' from.'

'Well, I've heard it said that good paymasters are usually lords of other men's purses, whoever they may be.' In the day's early light, Jack noticed the flecks of grey hair around Berry's temples, how the stamp of years was taking its toll. 'Would that be the coffee that Forge served me in your office?' he asked.

'Yeah, probably, if it was my office. You want some?'

Jack nodded, gave a deadpan look that Charlie Wei would have been proud of.

Berry continued as though he was suddenly voicing his private doubts. 'It's always seemed a bit odd that, from the time Wei had his accident an' got bought out, the mine decided to offer up its riches. We all thought that Charlie was jealous of Weaver's success, an' put it down to an unfortunate coincidence. The older you get though, the more you doubt those twists of fate. Maybe Charlie had good reason to think the way he did. Maybe I should have looked into it more. I need time,' he added, taking a deep breath. 'Give me a week. My word's still good about Tucson. One week for me to straighten things out here. You've waited all these years, a few more days won't make much difference.'

Jack considered a moment, then shook his head. Las Cruces trouble that hadn't been sorted during that time, should have been. Ongoing stuff would be the responsibility of Berry's successor. 'Thanks for the coffee, we're leaving within the hour,' he stated. 'An' that's my word.'

'Yeah, I thought you'd say that.' Berry chewed at his lip. He said nothing more, and Jack felt Raphaela's eyes on him, could almost hear the silent scream of distress.

'Perhaps you'll choke on it,' she muttered, topping up his cup with more steaming coffee.

A few silent minutes later soreness remained, but much of the ache had eased from Jack's skull and he went back to the bedroom. He took another double-handed splash of water across his face and buckled on his gunbelt. Then he walked out to the lean-to and saddled his claybank and the sheriff's mount. He was leading both horses back to the house, when Leo Forge rode in from the direction of town.

'So the sheriff's still here,' Forge said curtly, noting the saddles.

'Yeah. But he's getting ready not to be,' Jack returned the mayor's directness.

'We'll see about that.' Forge swung down and walked straight on past him towards the scullery side door.

Jack hitched the horses and went after him, idly wondering if the man split his time equally between the mayor's office, the sheriff's office and out there. He held open the scullery door as Forge spoke.

'There's been trouble, Lewis, an' I don't mean last night's ruckus or brawlin' in the saloon. Amos

85

Storey's been shot dead outside his own mine.'

'Amos Storey?' Berry echoed. He gave a despondent shake of his head and got to his feet as though required to do something. 'Who was it? The Weaver boys?'

'They were in town.' Forge gave nodding assent. 'They rode out in the early hours. McKrew says that's about the time Storey was killed. An hour or so later, maybe.'

'Robbery?'

'What else? Maybe there's some way of making a tally of the silver he's already mined. There's no register, sure as hell won't be any records, for us to go through.' Forge scowled, glanced at Jack, then looked back at Berry. 'We've been standing idle, Lew. We should have made a move earlier. It's lawless . . . out of hand, an' we've got to do something. Not for us, for the town, those who put us here. We let a bunch of land rats take the bank, an' ride away unscathed. That wouldn't have happened a year ago. For the killing alone, there'd be a string party off o' the Catwalk.'

'Yeah, I know.' Berry seemed to slouch further down into his chair, the years more clearly evident in his face. 'Truth is Leo, I've slowed up some,' he offered.

'You can only do so much, Lew,' Forge replied. 'I don't mean you've outlived your job. I mean that we, all of us, should have got tougher when the town started to boom. We all know that sudden wealth can be treacherous. Our law an' order's turned a blind eye. Lately we've even put a patch over it.'

Berry straightened his shoulders, attempted to look like the able sheriff. But he knew it was already too late. With Jack's arrival, the returning of his past life, a lot of marrow had been sucked from his bones.

'We'll ride out an' take a look at Storey's mine,' Forge decided bluntly. 'Maybe there's somethin' we can learn . . . get a lead on who did it.'

'You'll learn something, you arrogant son-of-a-bitch,' Jack rasped. 'He comes with me. Even if I have to slow one or two o' you down. And just for the record, I seem to recollect putting a pair o' those land rats you mentioned, back in the ground. That's not exactly *unscathed* in my book.'

They had overlooked, or disregarded Jack for a moment. When he moved into the scullery, the men appeared to be taken by surprise.

Forge swore, took a step back as the barrel of Jack's big Colt swung towards him. 'I'm a mayor, he's a sheriff, an' you're out o' your goddamn depth. Don't be a fool,' he barked. 'You'll get chased to the Pacific Ocean. I'll make sure of it.'

11

If Leo Forge had any doubts concerning the fierce determination that burned within Jack Calveron, there was none remaining. If he hadn't before fully understood the iron will that had brought him to Las Cruces, the ruthlessness of his cause, then he did now.

Jack had been badly wronged, but it was more than that. Serving your sentence was one thing, but it wasn't an affirmation that you hadn't committed the crime. A stigma had been placed upon his character, disgrace, for a US marshal who had traded on his integrity and sense of worth.

So, Forge continued to back off until he was against the wall, standing close alongside Raphaela, whose eyes burned with anger and frustration.

'I asked for a week,' Berry said, pushing himself up from his chair and edging towards the half open door. 'I didn't think it was too much to ask ... nothing to get shot for.'

Jack nodded coldly 'When I was in Redrock, I

asked for more bread. So they used a night-stick on me, an' I couldn't eat for a week. What you think's not worth spit.'

'I wanted to leave a clean town behind me, that's all,' Berry returned. 'You'd have me do otherwise, would you? You want this town to become the Tucson that you tried to tidy up? Maybe they'll get the feller, but if it's our customary posse, they'll likely string up the first man they see off the main street.'

'What the hell do you expect me to do about it? You said yourself it's *your* town, not mine.'

'With your help maybe we can lift the right man,' Berry suggested. 'If we impose hard-hitting punishment, make it frightening enough, the troublemakers will think twice.'

What Berry had said about Tucson suddenly got through to Jack, and he let the Colt drop to his side. 'From what I've learned so far, this Storey feller could've had good reason to get himself killed,' he said.

Berry looked across the scullery, meeting the hold of Jack's blue eyes. 'You might have heard otherwise, but Las Cruces ain't a nunnery an' nor's the sister towns. I've spent a few years trying to make the law work by evidence an' proof of misdeed, not by chance accusation.'

Jack took on the sheriff's statement, grinned incredulously at the sting of personal experience. 'Jeeesus Berry, you've picked up some mighty queer notions since we last met,' he said. 'If you'd been one o' them lay preachers, I'd say a full-blood convert.'

An audible breath escaped from Raphaela, a doubtful, muttered oath from Forge.

It was ten seconds before Jack pushed his Colt back into its holster. 'OK, just so long as we don't put together one of them chance, even contrived, accusations,' he accepted. 'We don't want any o' that. We'll ride up to that mine and take a look. But I'm warning you now, Berry, if this mess isn't cleared up in one week, I'll shoot you dead, an' go back on my own, no question.'

'Yeah, well, that's got the legal niceties out o' the way,' Leo Forge said turning on his heel. 'Let's get goin'.'

The Weaver mine was back in the hills to the northeast of Las Cruces, two miles off the trail to Mimbres. Erskine Weaver had built it up considerably from Charlie Wei's time, and before declaring a significant strike of high grade ore. If there were any questions about the validity of the strike, there were few local folk of a mind to voice them, save Charlie Wei, himself.

Weaver stood big, though without as much lard and muscle as he'd once carried. He was a dominant man and an ambitious one. He was scornful of the law, and, despite what might be described as overconfident, had one powerful and ever present advantage in his efforts to grab at the wealth of Las Cruces: the men on Weaver's payroll knew little of scruples. They were prepared to do his bidding without question, eager to fatten their pockets from

regular hand outs and bonuses. But Weaver brooked
no argument. Any man who voiced or showed
dissent, wasn't prepared to use a gun when required,
got summarily disposed of. 'Gone to the Pecos' was
no idle expression.

Many of the drifters, grubbers and owlhoots who
came to Las Cruces to make an easy dollar came
under the eye of Weaver or his top railer, Goose
Hollister. They were allowed to continue in their
activities only so long as it suited, and not ever at
Weaver's expense. The man had become a law
outside of the law, operating with the arrogance of
someone who couldn't be touched.

The arrival of Fausto Salt, and the subsequent
bank robbery were palpable thorns in Weaver's side.
Not only personal cash bank deposits, but dollars
had been taken that he considered his to exploit. It
was a crime which wasn't going unpunished and,
since the mayor and the posse had been unable to
catch up with the outlaws, Weaver had vowed to
handle it himself. But at the moment, from the
gloom of the mine's site cabin, there was another
matter that needed his consideration.

'We didn't want to kill him,' Gaff Oaks said. 'We
did just like you said, boss. We waited till just on dark,
back from the mine in the gully. There was no light
in the shack, an' no smoke comin' from the chimney.
We figured he must have been headed for town.'

'Instead, he was lying low waiting for you,' Weaver
proposed, tapping his thick fingers together.

'He came at us with a goddamn scattergun. I had

to shoot him.' Oaks gave his explanation simple, the way Weaver liked it. 'We hauled out what we could. It weren't easy in the dark . . . couldn't tell what was pay dirt, what wasn't. There's rats in them black holes, rattlers too.'

'You reckon maybe *they* told him you were coming?' Weaver continued.

Oaks shrugged. 'That hound of his probably got hackled up.'

'Hound? You knew he had a dog up there?'

'Yeah, but we was told it was some lame old mut. It came at us like a banshee, spittin' an' snarlin' like it was goin' to tear our legs off.' Oaks grimaced, then grinned a little at the recollection. 'We near blew its head off.'

Thoughtfully, Weaver leaned back in his chair. 'Hmm, maybe it was the dog that warned him, maybe not,' he speculated. 'But we got what we set out for. So, now get your stories straight, lest that fool sheriff comes nosing around.'

Oaks nodded confidently as he went over the prepared alibi. 'Me an' the boys were here mindin' the stock, guardin' our own property. We didn't go no place at all, boss. We were doin' our jobs like we were told, an' that's the whole truth.'

Goose Hollister stepped forward from where he was at the door, listening. 'That's right, an' the rest of us were in town the whole time,' he said, with a scheming grin. 'We made sure everyone knew it.'

'But the sheriff didn't bother you . . . didn't show his face?' Weaver asked.

'No.' Hollister's eyes narrowed. 'I guess that bullet he took must have slowed him down some.'

Reassured, Weaver smirked and rubbed his hands together. Things were going along smoothly just as he planned. No hitches, no problems, apart from the bunch who'd ridden in to raid the bank.

'Goose' – Weaver held Hollister with a steady stare – 'there *is* something else . . . another job for you. You were near at hand when the bank was robbed, and you got a good look at them who pulled it.'

Hollister nodded, listened up as Weaver continued.

'I got word that they doubled back, which means that if they did, they're probably hiding out somewhere in town. I want you to find 'em and let me know where they are.'

'Yeah, sure, I can do that,' Hollister said, but looked puzzled. 'What you aimin' to do?'

'Get my dollars back,' Weaver grinned. 'In this case though, I got a feeling that the saying's easier than the doing. But once I've got the money, I'll figure out what's to be done with *them*. I haven't got to where I am today, Goose, by folk believing that what's theirs is theirs forever. Maybe them big ol' Pecos catfish need more meat.'

Hollister chuckled. Weaver had the town in his pocket, was getting so influential, that for one reason or another, even the sheriff couldn't touch him. The man had already set his sights on the Las Cruces Depository, all he needed was an effective strategy before he took action. In Hollister's opinion, the day was fast approaching when Erskine Weaver owned Las Cruces, Santa Rita and Mimbres, lock stock and barrel.

The big, iron-bound Weaver safes were packed with silver deposits all right, but it was a lot more than the Weaver mine had ever yielded, or was ever likely to. There was much low gossip, but with the exception of Charlie Wei, no one dared suggest that something was off beam, or make an outright accusation.

Hollister had seen Weaver associating with Leo Forge and the rest of the town council, was aware that one time he'd even been invited to join their ranks, help with the general administration of the town. The Chinaman's suspicions had prompted the sheriff to make a few enquiries, but it wasn't too deep an investigation and consequently didn't amount to much. To all appearances, Weaver's business was exactly as he claimed: he had a rich silver mine, and employed men who worked hard. Each and every one of them deserved the right to swing the doors, and if they happened to step out of line now and again, it should be accepted as a question of balance.

'They're a rough, tough bunch,' Hollister had once heard Weaver conceding to Lewis Berry. 'They have to be. I've some valuable property and I hire men fit to protect an' run it. If they want to kick up their heels, I'm not going to chastise 'em for it, and I'd be grateful if you didn't either.'

'So, you'd better ride,' Weaver now told Hollister. 'Get back here as soon as you can. Whatever you do, don't make any move that might alarm 'em. I want most of everything they stole. I *don't* want 'em to get panicked an' stash it away.'

Weaver stood watching from the doorway as Hollister crossed the yard to the stock huts. There were always fresh, well-looked-after horses to take out. Where speed of business was concerned, Weaver believed in contingency, and the animals were vital transport. He waited until Hollister had saddled up and ridden out, then he turned back to Oaks.

'I'll take a look at that ore, now,' he said. 'I want to make sure it's worth hiding. The law's bound to come by with questions.'

Alarm showed for a moment on Gaff Oaks's face. 'Sheriff Berry? You think he'd have the guts to come up here?'

'Why should he need guts to pay us a visit?' Weaver snapped back. 'Besides, that ain't a commodity he's known to be short of . . . not while he's packin' a badge. No, don't go making that mistake. Maybe he hasn't reasoned it out, but I'm sure not taking any goddamn chances.'

Oaks grunted an understanding, then led the way through the excavated detritus, across the clearing to the shored up mouth of the mine. It wasn't long after daybreak and the first shift had just begun. Two coupled trucks were being wheeled along a narrow track, dipping on the slight incline, then vanishing into the gloom of the pit beyond. A small group of shovellers and bucket men called a greeting to Weaver who raised his hand in acknowledgement.

'If appearances are anything to go by, perhaps one day I really will hit pay dirt,' Weaver muttered drily.

Oaks looked around him as if to figure out Weaver's thoughts. Then he lifted a pair of jack lanterns, held them before him as they ducked to enter the mineshaft.

12

It wasn't a surprise to Jack Calveron that Raphaela insisted on riding with her stepfather to Amos Storey's silver mine. Lewis Berry had his ribs bound up from the bank robbery, his face hadn't resumed its normal ruddiness, and he winced continually at the pain that still chewed into him. Added to this was a pervading fear that Jack wouldn't honour his agreement, that he'd compel the sheriff to accompany him back to Tucson.

Frequently, Raphaela turned to look back at Jack, then shifting her glance quickly between Leo Forge and Berry who rode beside her. She seemed to be wanting some sort of sign, some assurance that everything would be all right. It was Berry's testimony that Jack wanted, she thought. But she also knew that Jack wouldn't countenance a statement without Berry making it in person, confessing at the scene of the crime, saying the words. Then she got to thinking about what would happen to Berry after that; how Jack would regard her stepfather's prospects.

Jack was riding well in the rear. He was ruefully considering the animosity directed towards him when Raphaela dropped back to ride alongside.

'You're a strange man, Jack Calveron. I wouldn't have had you pegged as a ruthless one,' she said. 'It seems such a waste . . . so unimaginative,' she added, when Jack didn't respond immediately.

'I don't think I'm ruthless,' Jack replied after another wait. 'Surely you'd all be dead, if I was?'

'I wasn't suggesting you were a killer,' she responded fiercely. 'Have you ever heard the saying, what's done is done?'

After another long pause, Jack gave a slight nod of his head. 'Yes, ma'am, I have. It was the argument of a wretch who'd just stove some poor barkeep's head in.'

'I was thinking about the victim's feelings . . . the forgiveness of someone who's suffered.'

'Ah well, you don't get much o' that inside Redrock Stockade, ma'am.'

'Hasn't there been anyone *since then* to make you feel different? There must have been someone,' Raphaela suggested with a touch of irritation. Then colour touched her cheeks the way it had in her room when her hand had rested on his arm.

'No, ma'am. Not from before, either.'

'My name's Raphaela. I'm not a ma'am.'

'Yes, ma'am, I didn't mean—'

'I know, forget it,' Raphaela interrupted. 'But people change. Isn't it best sometimes to leave things as they are, without digging up the past?'

'Listen . . . Raphaela, I'm not digging up the past. As far as I'm concerned, it's still there rotting on the surface.'

'Well, just remember, this isn't Tucson . . . Arizona, even. Folk here don't know you, and nothing about what happened back there. There'll be no finger pointing or tongues wagging behind your back. So why not simply forget it and start over?'

'Because I'm the one it happened to . . . the price they had me pay. That's something I'm not likely to *simply* forget.' Jack's words were quiet and cold. 'Maybe when it's all over . . . maybe. Meantime, I know you've got cause, but I'm getting tired of listening to your churchy mores.'

'Thank you for that. Offensive is something else I can add to ruthless,' she muttered.

Raphaela turned away and nudged her horse, heeling it to catch up with the others. They all rode on and she didn't look back again. Jack noted the sag of her shoulders, sensed the misery that filled her.

Despite her present unhappiness, Raphaela was a good-looking girl, filled with a fiery vitality. Jack felt as though his blood had warmed a degree or two and, for a short moment, wondered about changing his mind, letting the past turn to dust behind him. Like she'd said, he wasn't known in Las Cruces, the neighbour country. It was a fact that no one, save for her and Forge, had any real idea of what had happened back in Tucson, He could forget Berry; he wasn't likely to go telling anyone. But how long would it be before the urge to right the wrong came flooding back? Perhaps it wouldn't, but he'd never know for sure. He'd never rest peaceable.

Jack felt a sudden and quite unexpected wave of tiredness and he closed his eyes for a while. On the horns of a dilemma, he didn't know if it was weariness from the chase, common sense or rising compassion, even. He guessed it was probably all of that, and with Raphaela figuring highly.

It was a prospector called Longhorn who found the body of Amos Storey. He was coming from the foothills around Mimbres, making camp late evening, when the trail became too treacherous for his burros to follow. He rolled himself in his blanket, totally unaware there was a silver mine close to where he was spending the night. He woke at daybreak to see the shack that was Storey's home. When his belly growled with hunger, he thought he'd try his luck for some beans and bacon.

Amos Storey had been dead all night, his body lying where it had fallen, twisted and stiff, powdered with a light rime. Agitated, Longhorn huffed and puffed back to his animals and hurried them straight down to Las Cruces. Along with anyone who would listen to his tale, he called out Doc McKrew. Then, muttering and cursing his luck, he sought out the Paraiso saloon to try for a messenger's reward.

From his window above the street, Fausto Salt was stirred by the early activity. Drowsy, he raised himself from the unfamiliar comfort of his bed, the plump soft curl of a saloon girl's arm. Pulling on his slouch hat, he watched the arrival of Jack Calveron and company, wondering what the fuss was about.

From behind a curtain that screened him from Salt's personal activities, Gethin Pintura shivered in the chill air. Standing from further back in the room, he looked down into the street, observing the sheriff and the star pinned to his chest, the smarter dressed mayor. His gaze rested for a moment longer on the tall figure of Jack Calveron, then he saw the girl.

Women had always been a weakness of Gethin Pintura, a fact which was well known to Salt, who accepted it as innate. Pintura had promised self-restraint because of Salt's plans, but the sight of Raphaela now drove all such matters from his head, and he stood fascinated by her, drinking in every feature.

Minutes later, he was still watching as the group rode from town. They carried no packs and no bedrolls, so he concluded that they would be back. He had no idea who the girl might be, but decided he was going to find out, grinning at the coarse, carnal thoughts that drifted through his head. No longer shivering, he looked at his reflection in a hanging mirror. His eyes were prime bright, but with the hair cutting he'd endured at the hands of Salt, it was as though a younger persona had been revealed, revealing more swaggering and eager desires.

13

Fausto Salt was delighted with the progress made by Pintura. The fact that he'd contacted and made friends with one of the Las Cruces Depository guards was his high card in the hand he intended to play. He listened carefully to Pintura's detailed account of his meeting with Minty Book, and Book's promise to show him the inside of the depository.

Pintura smiled uncertainly at the slap of Salt's hand on his shoulder, and Wallace Trench grinned at the obvious satisfaction.

'Gimme a kiss, you little beauty,' he teased, pinching a clean-shaven cheek between his thumb and forefinger.

'Hah, but it worked. You did real well, Geth,' Salt encouraged. 'All you have to do now, is win over this Book fellow. Find out the times that those guards go on an' off duty. We've got to know how many there are, an' just whereabouts inside the bank they're stationed. There'll be silver an' gold in the safes, but it's their cash we want. An' remember, we don't want to go in *after* the miners make their withdrawals. Do you reckon you can get all that without arousing suspicion?'

'Book the beef-wit,' Pintura grunted, as he swiped Trench's hand away. 'He don't have the brains to suspect anything, except when his gut's growlin'.'

'Yeah, but I don't want to live on a maybe. Just don't get up anyone's nose. Do like I told you. Be friendly. Don't go snooping. An' if *he* wants to give you a kiss or a cuddle . . . let him.'

'If he comes close enough for that, I'll rip his face off,' Pintura sneered.

Salt smiled encouragingly and waved him out of the room.

Pintura was comfortable with the advice of his boss, though his mind was still set on his earthy thoughts of the morning. He continued to picture Raphaela, her long, flowing brown hair, her ankle boots, and it wasn't long before his mind wandered wildly off track again. He crossed the street, walking slowly towards the place where he'd eaten stew with Minty Book the evening before. He looked ahead to the Paraiso saloon, recalled the bullet that nearly blew the top off the guard's thick skull. Then the thought of a Pass whiskey or two made him swallow miserably. His thoughts snapped back to Raphaela and he cursed again because it was the wrong time. He told himself that she was just another woman, another pretty face and probably no different from all the others. After all, he'd had nothing more than a glimpse of her and that was from a distance. But there was something about her, something that wouldn't allow his mind to still. His hands were sweating and he rubbed his palms against his upper arms as he walked on. He saw the line of character-less doorways ahead of him and remembered the moment from the previous night; an overpainted mouth, the cheap perfume, the tempting figure that Book had dragged him away from. He bit his bottom lip and cursed at the promises he'd made to Fausto Salt. His copperhead black eyes flashed as he pressed the toe of his boot against the sill of the first door. He cursed again, rapping his knuckles urgently as frustration overwhelmed him.

The town was well awake and running when Gethin Pintura returned. He crossed the lobby without attracting attention, went directly upstairs to his room. His desire was still running high, but, until thoughts of Raphaela stirred him again, somewhat assuaged.

He closed the door behind him, went straight to a pitcher of water in Salt's side of the room and removed his shirt. He stood with his back to the door, taking a second or two to turn around when it swung open.

'Gethin, you don't normally bathe this early in the week,' Fausto Salt exclaimed. But he'd already seen the scratches that ran lividly across Pintura's shoulder blades. 'What the hell's goin' on?' he demanded. 'I said you was to go an' talk with that bank guard. I said you was to stay away from women. For Chris'sake, you look as though you've been in a ring with ol' grizzler.'

Pintura edged away. He flinched at the withering stare that blazed from Wallace Trench who was now standing behind Salt.

'If you've gone an' took some woman down one o' them alleyways. . . .' Salt was seething with anger. 'You've could've undone everythin' we planned. Don't you realize the town won't stand for this sort o' thing? What if she goes to the sheriff? What if they come looking for you? What then, goddamnit?'

'They won't, Fausto.' Pintura found his voice, shook his head in protest against Salt's rage. 'It was in one o' them cat rooms. The ones with a red light. She was a chippy.'

Salt stepped forward, crashed the back of his hand full across Pintura's mouth. 'I trusted you Geth, an' you let me down.' His face darkened and his eyes flashed more anger as he curled his hand around the butt of his Colt. 'I ought to shoot you here an' now for what you've done,' he fumed.

'If it was up to me, I'd slice off your gonads before I did that,' Trench snarled his own accompanying threat.

'Clean yourself up an' get dressed. We'll talk about this later,' Salt snapped, as he turned away. 'You follow on behind me,' he ordered Trench. 'I'm goin' down to take a look at that bank.'

Salt stepped out into the bright daylight of the street. Horse-drawn vehicles of every description

moved backwards and forwards in dogged proces-
sion as the day's business started up. Salt walked
quickly, the anger still etched in the lines of his face,
clear in the muttering of profanities and dire threats.

He was heading for the Las Cruces Depository, but
there was a store he'd seen earlier that, with a bit of
luck, held the key to his plan. A painted sign hanging
out above the walkway proclaimed the shop to be
Fairley's Stock Supplies. He paused to think for a
moment then entered, ringing a cow bell above the
door.

'Good mornin'.' Pat Fairley was standing behind a
long, deep counter. He was labelling bottles, waiting
for the first customer.

'Good mornin' to you,' Salt replied. 'I'm lookin'
for a sleepin' draught. Peyote, Jimson, Cactus Juice,
anythin' to tranquillize a prize Hereford bull. I've got
to do somethin' he won't like.'

Fairley eyed Salt. 'Hmm, you can get most o' that
from the Paraiso,' he said. 'But I got some Cordial
Cure that'll make a buffler sleep for a week. It's powerful stuff, but it'll cost you a full dollar.'

'That's fine. Add a spoonful o' black-strap; I don't
want the brute to spit it out,' he added, dragging up
an affable smile. 'I don't want it smellin' bad, either.'

Fairley gave Salt another doubtful look. 'Picky is
he, this prize bull o' yours?'

'Yeah, he's real fussy,' Salt continued with the false-
hood. 'An' real valuable.'

Let's hope it's yours, was Fairley's flawed thought
as he gave the small bottle a shake.

Salt allowed himself a tight smile. His annoyance with Pintura was weakening. Despite Pintura's carnal blunder, there was now a fair chance his plan might succeed. He might have to reconsider certain aspects, but he was on track.

He snapped a dollar on to the counter and tucked the potent physic carefully into his shirt pocket. 'There, we wouldn't want to lose it,' he said, and thanked Fairley.

Five minutes later, he nodded civilly as he walked past the depository guard. Inside the bank, he stood casually for a long searching look around, taking in the tellers' cages and the cluster of desks at the rear, the entrance to the secure area of safes and vaults. He mentally recorded the scene, then calmly left the building in the belief that no one had taken any notice of him.

14

The Storey mine was deserted, save for a rising jay. Jack Calveron walked his claybank mare to a patch of shade, stood watching as Leo Forge, Berry and Raphaela dismounted. Forge had a quick look around him, then wandered to the mouth of the mine. He stared at the ground a moment, peered into the inner gloom then returned to speak to Jack.

'Seems to me that if you're in such a fired-up hurry to leave, you could try helping. At least get off your goddamn horse an' show some interest.' He fumbled in a top pocket for a cigar, bit at it, spat and lit up before going on. 'You give the sheriff a few days, and then sit your saddle an' watch.'

'I gave him a week,' Jack replied. 'You figuring on me doing his job? I seem to recollect someone saying I've no authority in this neck o' the woods.'

Forge scowled, dragged on the smoke. 'I always thought the law was law. Same for its officers.'

'Like when it's on your side, eh Mr Mayor?'

Berry intervened then, quickly, as Forge's displeasure started to show. He caught hold of the man's arm, looking earnestly to Jack. 'We'll take a look around in that gully behind the diggings.' He motioned to the horses, letting go of Forge and starting to remount as he spoke. 'Amos Storey wouldn't have kept much cash here, even if he had any. The only valuable would be his ore. If they killed him to get *that*, they could have travelled light.'

Jack wondered how much they were talking about. He didn't think it could possibly be more than what a couple of men could stash into their saddle pockets. But what Berry said made some sort of sense, and quarrelling with the mayor wouldn't get them anywhere. He'd made a deal and had best stick with it. Furthemore, if he did intend to leave when the week was up, helping the sheriff meant he wouldn't have to kill him.

'While you're looking through that gully, I'll take a look along the ridges,' he decided categorically. 'Our mayor can nose around the mine, and Raphaela can check out the shack. Maybe there's something to learn, if you can overcome the fragrance.'

Jack rode slowly, letting the mare follow its own course as it climbed the ridges that rose up from either side of the mine. It was steep, rugged ground, and any ox cart or mule train would be hard pressed to find a navigable trail. The trail down and back to Las Cruces was better defined, widened through use, allowing the transport of ore to the assay houses and banks, rail and stage connections to the East. Though the Storey mine was a way back from the road, the trail linked it pretty well.

A few minutes later, Forge emerged from the mine shaft to say that it didn't look like there was any ore stacked for transport. 'There's signs it was piled there though. Unless it's in the cabin, it's been cleared out,' he said.

Jack looked to Raphaela who shook her head in answer. Then he turned to Berry. 'How about the gully? Did you find anything?'

'Yeah. Looks like there was three or four riders. They were riding light, or it was two of 'em, loaded up. Take your pick.'

'Either way, it looks like they took out something.' Jack scanned the surrounding hills and frowned. 'I don't understand. Perhaps they were collecting from more than just the Storey mine; perhaps it was cash they wanted.' His bright-blue eyes held Berry, probing silently as though for an explanation the sheriff couldn't put into words. 'A while back you suggested you'd had some thoughts about who was behind all this. Perhaps now's the time to name names,' Jack suggested, noting the man's unease.

'Erskine Weaver.' Berry glanced sideways at Forge who grunted for some reason, making ready to swear. 'I've got no proof, of course. All I know is, is that whenever his men are havin' a good time in town, there's something bad happenin' *outside* of it.'

'Yeah, the thing a lot of prudent lawmen don't believe in . . . coincidence,' Jack said. 'You're saying one bunch keeps you busy while another does Weaver's dirty work?'

Berry nodded. 'Other than that, there's only Charlie Wei's claims an' allegations. Since McKrew brought Amos Storey back to town, he's been even more worked up. But most folk still reckon it's a personal axe he's grinding.'

'That doesn't mean to say it's not true. If we found the stolen ore, that would be encouraging . . . more than a stove-up old Chinaman's vinegary claim.'

'How would we prove the ore belonged to Storey?' Berry asked. 'It don't come with an owner's label stamped on it.'

'Yeah, I know. But if we want some answers, we've got to go and push for 'em,' Jack responded energetically. 'While the mayor rides back to town with Raphaela, you and me ride over and have a talk with this Weaver feller. If he's got nothing to hide, he's got nothing to worry about.'

'Hmm, Erskine Weaver don't often get talked about like that,' Berry grinned unsmilingly. 'I suggest you ease up on the pushing, otherwise we'll both get shot from our saddles.'

'I doubt that,' Jack said. 'He'll want to prove his innocence. He wants the law alongside him. That way he gets to carry on.'

Forge grunted his displeasure but Jack was resolute. He had methods that the mayor of Las Cruces probably wouldn't approve of, that Raphaela certainly wouldn't. As they rode off, Raphaela turned around as Jack was sure she would, and he raised his hand as a response. For the shortest moment, he was stirred with regret, then he pushed such feelings from his head and confronted Berry.

'When we get to Weaver's place, you'll let me do the talking. You've got a gun, but don't start anything unless you have to. You're a law officer, remember. Weaver's going to be plenty sore when he finds out why we're riding on to his property. Do you think you're up to it?'

Sheriff Berry made no comment, simply fixed Jack with a steely stare. Then he pointed the way, swung his mount in behind the claybank as Jack took the lead.

Deep in their own thoughts, they rode until the silence was broken by Jack. 'Assuming they've got it, how do you figure they'll dispose of the ore?' he asked, looking sideways at the sheriff.

'Stockpile it,' Berry stated emphatically. 'Then, as the heat dies down, increase their yield to the mills. That way it looks like they struck a rich seam . . . *another* rich seam.'

Jack nodded. He had a clearer picture now of an illicit operation, abeit an unproven one. Weaver had a mine that evidently was providing him with a perfect front for his real business. He had no problem disposing of the ore, dividing it between the crushing plants at Santa Rita and the mills outside of Las Cruces. Jack didn't think that making an attestable case against him would be easy.

Berry pointed, and Jack looked ahead to where a track broke from the hills to meet with the road to

Mimbres. Two miles further east, nestling in the the ridged foothills, they saw the cabin, stock huts and saddle horses of the Weaver mine.

Around the mouth of a heavily propped mine entrance, a group of men were dragging out two ore trucks from the interior. Rocks were heaped up on either side of the track, and a freight wagon was being loaded in preparation for its trip to the mill.

As Jack and Lewis Berry cautiously approached, a big man emerged in the doorway of the near cabin and stood watching them. He wasn't armed, but his stance wasn't a welcoming one.

'That's him . . . Erskine Weaver,' Berry said, deciding to dismount.

Jack remained in the saddle. He knew that was the safest, most intimidating place to be when approaching an unfamiliar party.

In the gloom of the cabin, two men were standing behind Weaver. Jack quickly guessed what their instructions would have been in the case of trouble, realized that he and Berry had been watched from the moment they'd turned off the Mimbres trail. Weaver eyed Berry for a moment, then took a more shrewd look at Jack, as Jack knew he would. The man trusted his wits, what he saw for himself, and Jack returned the chilly stare of judgement.

He flexed himself in the saddle, made himself at ease. In Jack Calveron, Sheriff Berry had gained himself an ally who was undoubtedly an imposing figure.

'We're here to look around,' Jack said. 'I'm

hoping we don't have to mess with your business.' He spoke up before Berry could get a word out, went on before Weaver could put together a protest. 'You see, a man was robbed last night after being shot dead. Because of it, there's rumours. Rumours we've got to listen to.'

Weaver muttered a curse. 'I've got a feeling that telling you to get lost, wouldn't cut much ice, mister.' Weaver tried a tight smile, then, without taking his eyes off Jack, and in an incredibly fast movement, he flicked his hand forward as a signal to his men.

Gaff Oaks hunkered down. At the same instant, the other man brought up a shotgun.

But Jack was ahead of them. He was expecting such a move and his hand had already swept up his big Colt in one fast, effortless movement. He fired twice, the echoes reverberating like crazy around the high rising ridges. His first bullet hit Oaks high in the chest. The impact lifted the man from his crouch, staggering him back into the legs of his colleague before he crumpled. The second bullet punched into the belly of Oaks's cohort. Within a second of each other, both men hit the ground lifeless.

Jack cursed to himself, incredulous that the prudent, vigilant Erskine Weaver he'd heard so much about, had got himself such ineffective protection.

The action had been sudden and bloody, taking Berry by surprise, if not Weaver.

'Christ, did you have to do that?' Berry rasped out, with the echoes of the shots still echoing in the distance.

'No. But on Mr Weaver's say so, we'd both be dead if I hadn't. Ain't that so, Mr Weaver?' Jack returned.

'Who the hell are you, feller? What the hell you want?' Weaver snarled back.

Jack climbed down from his mare, shifted his Colt to point directly at Weaver. 'I'm Jack Calveron, an' we're here to look for the ore that was stolen from old Amos Storey. You're smart enough to know that, so go and tell your men that if anyone gets in our way, they'll likely get carried back to town with them two. You can go with 'em if you like,' he added icily.

No sooner had Jack given his warning than Weaver's men came running from the mine entrance. But they came to a faltering halt when they saw their boss under threat from Jack, and Sheriff Berry checking out two dead men at the cabin. Like a lot of men who accepted fighting wages, they weren't blindly committed after the first death, and Weaver waved them back as Jack's Colt now pressed tellingly against his spine.

'You'll have to light the way,' Jack said, motioning for Berry to move ahead and take a lantern.

They had only just entered the mine when trouble sprang from the shadows. From beside an upright piling, a man leaped out and slammed the lamp from Berry's extended hand. A second hurled himself at Jack, who reeled backwards, raising his gun hand, but making no attempt to fire.

Thinking he was in grave danger, about to die, Weaver shouted in alarm. 'It's me, you idiots. Stand away. Let us through.'

But it was a tad late and Jack twisted away. He pressed his back up against the wall of the pit, evading the full force of his attacker. The man lost his balance and, as he tripped forward, Jack chopped down hard with his Colt. He heard the dull thud, felt the sickening collapse of flesh and bone low on the side of the man's head. He gasped with the effort, pushed the Colt back into his holster as he leant down, grabbing at the man's jacket to drag him aside.

In the gloom and low light from the fallen lantern, he looked ahead, giving out more appropriate curses. Berry was on one knee, ramming a man's face hard into the shale between the narrow truck rails.

Jack took a quick step forward as Weaver looked to be making a getaway back to the mine entrance. He swung a long looping fist hard and low into the big man's side, who stumbled forward gasping with pain.

'You're not missing out on this,' Jack seethed. Then he turned back for Berry, reaching out to help him back to standing. 'It was your idea,' he pointed out. 'I was all for riding on.'

Looking past Jack, Berry was about to say something when they both heard the nearby yells and wound-up curses.

Weaver's workforce had returned, and Jack realized he'd got it wrong. The miners had quickly considered the odds, were returning, more confident, to the aid of their boss. *Too much to goddamn lose*, he thought cynically, as he saw them rushing at the tunnel entrance.

They came brandishing shovels and pick axes. Most of them were armed with an assortment of holstered, workmanlike revolvers, but were reluctant to shoot into the dangerous confines of the mine. As they drew closer, the angry miners were trying to see through the gloom, past the weak yellowy light of the spilled lantern.

Jack and Lewis Berry stood facing each other. They were up against the pit walls, taking deep, steadying breaths.

'Huh, you said Weaver wants the law alongside him,' Berry rasped as he drew his Colt. 'How the hell d'you figure that?'

'This is for appearance's sake,' Jack returned with a grim smile. 'They've all been told to make it look like there's something to protect.'

'So what do we do?'

'Try to stay alive, you son-of-a-bitch,' Jack snapped as the miners rushed headlong towards them.

15

Erskine Weaver knew that making any defiant move against Jack's purpose would be a waste of time, probably cost him his life. Slumped on the floor of his own mine, he clasped an arm to the sharp pain in his side and gagged. Watery-eyed, he watched Jack looking to Sheriff Berry as his payroll miners bore down on them. He turned to the ground and spat, vowed that if his men didn't tear them apart, he'd somehow have to kill both of them himself.

Jack met the first of the storming mob with an iron tie bar he picked up from beside the rail track. Hefting one end with both hands he swung the rod in an arc, stepping forward doggedly to confront the angry miners. He caught the first man across his shoulder, and he went down screaming in agony. His eyes blazing, Jack stepped on his writhing body, before lunging into the next attacker. He smashed the man's knee cap, dropping to the ground with him as he brought up the bar under the jaw of the

118

next man. At the sickening impact, Jack cursed aloud, thrust the bar forward into the belly of the nearest of the next two men.

'I'm all in, Berry,' he yelled. 'Where the hell are you?'

'Right beside you, an' I'm takin' this one.' With that, Berry lashed out with his boot, then struck the other man full in the face with the frame of his Colt. The man grunted, and dropped his shovel. His hands reached for his shattered nose and mouth as he stumbled on into the deeper gloom of the mine.

With Berry at his side, Jack made a move for the mine entrance. The few remaining miners turned and ran for fear of being injured.

It was a combined force that drove Weaver's mining crew into retreat; that and the fear of being badly hurt. As the last man fled back into the open, Jack dropped the tie bar, stood gasping for breath at the mine entrance.

Berry drew the back of his hand across his lips. 'I reckon they'll have a rethink about comin' back. You don't always need a gun then?' he rasped.

'How to break stones and bones was about the only practical lesson I came out of Redrock with. An' you didn't fare so badly, considering you're walking wounded,' Jack replied grimly, motioning Berry back into the tunnel. 'Now, let's get on with what we came for. Any more resistance though, and someone gets a bullet.'

Erskine Weaver had staggered to his feet. He was

standing bent, his arms hanging loose at his sides making low, threatening noises. Jack paid no heed, picking up the lantern and pushing him ahead. They didn't have to go too far along the mine shaft before coming up against the rock and hard dirt face of the mountain. To one side, a tunnel veered off sharply into the deep, unlit darkness.

'Here it is.' Jack raised the lamp, moved it so its glow fell on the ore that had been tipped in neat piles either side of the tracks. The light caught the dull grey glow of silver, and Jack grunted with satisfaction. 'I'm no expert, but I'd say *this* is Storey's ore,' he declared. 'Here's where it meets the soil that's dug from the end of *that* tunnel . . . where it's mixed and loaded on to the trucks.'

'You can't prove that,' Weaver said, offering a small degree of argument.

'No, but an assayer might be able to,' Berry joined in. 'Like Jack, silver mining's not my speciality, but I'd say the silver in them two deposits doesn't match up. I'd say Old Charlie Wei's spot on. This mine o' yours is nothing more than a great pile of rock an' dirt. That's what I'd say, Mr Weaver.'

Beads of sweat appeared along Weaver's top lip, his eyes shifting with unease. 'There's no one can prove where that ore came from, an' you know it.' He gave a quick glance towards Berry, then, to clear any retaliatory blow that might come at him, edged a pace away from Jack.

'We'll take a handful anyway.' Jack nodded briefly to Berry. 'Nothing like evidence, eh, Sheriff?' He stooped to pick up some small pieces of ore, tucking them safely inside his shirt. 'We'll get some tests done, and we'll have a man out here to check out the vein you're working . . . if you can call it that.' He laid a withering stare on Weaver. 'I guess you know what to expect if you try and put a stop to it,' he warned.

As they rode on to the Las Cruces trail, Lewis Berry shook his head. 'You sure threw a scare into him. He'll be staggering around fearful of his own shadow. He's just met his nemesis, not his friend.'

'A tad like you, eh, Berry?'

'It's different. I've given myself up, *he* hasn't. An' I'm not so sure about the assay business. It sounds good, but I don't see how it can prove anything.'

'That's because it can't.' Jack grinned wryly. 'And *I'm* not so sure about him being fearful of his own shadow. You don't change a man like Weaver that quick. But it'll give him another belly-ache of worry, perhaps bring him into the open.'

Berry thought about it. Uncertain, he glanced back, saw the isolated figure of Weaver glaring after them. He flinched inwardly at the thought of Weaver's next move. Even without his two hired guns, it would be a different outcome when the man had better armed his workers, especially those who had been hurt. When he had inspired them with his own lust for retaliation, they would be riding on Las Cruces. 'I can feel his spleen from here,' Berry said. 'They'll likely be riding before the day's much older.'

'I hope he's learned there's some places it's best not to,' Jack added sharply.

16

After his look around the impressive Las Cruces Depository, and with Wallace Trench back in close attendance, Fausto Salt headed back to his hotel room. He had a long talk with Gethin Pintura and, when he was through, Pintura knew exactly what was to be done. Salt spoke briskly and concisely, letting Pintura know that he wouldn't tolerate any more indiscretions. 'Are you listenin' to me, Geth?' he demanded. 'You take a goddamn detour like you did last time . . . you even *think* about it, an' I'll do like Trench says. You *comprendez?*'

On the walkway opposite, partly concealed by shadow, a tall, slope-shouldered man stood watching the room where Salt explained his plan. His sharp eyes had already witnessed a bunch of men shooting their way out of the Santa Rita Development Bank, riding hell-for-leather to get clear of town. He had watched Fausto Salt make his way from the Prosperity Hotel to the supply store, then on to the depository. He had even intimidated Pat Fairley to find out about the potion that Salt had purchased from him.

Goose Hollister wasn't over gifted with wit or inge-
nuity, but he was inquisitive, possessing the
watch-and-tell way of thinking, much valued by his
boss, Erskine Weaver. He recognized Salt and Trench
as two of the men who had carried out the bank
robbery, and he'd wondered, as Weaver had, if they
were back in Las Cruces for a more rewarding prize.
At the moment, it was beginning to look like that
prize was none other than the outwardly impreg-
nable Las Cruces Depository. When they intended to
do it, Hollister had no idea. He had pieced together
a notion as to *how*, but that was all, and something for
Weaver himself to ponder on.

Hollister untied the reins of his mount from the
hitch rail outside of the beef and biscuit house, and
rode unconcernedly back along the main street. He
travelled at a steady pace until he was clear of the
town limits, then he dug in his heels. There was
going to be trouble, but it was Erskine Weaver who
would know how to handle it.

While Goose Hollister was heading back to the
Weaver mine, Gethin Pintura strolled to the depository to renew his acquaintance with Minty Book. He
carried Salt's sleeping draught in his pocket, but he
was doubtful. 'As sure as God made little green
apples,' Salt had said, but in spite of his high opinion
of the man, it was himself that had to carry out the
task and he had misgivings.

Book greeted Pintura with an affable grin. He

wasn't forgetting how Pintura had knocked him clear of the bullets that came erupting from in and around the Paraiso the previous evening. He knew the youngster's quick thinking had likely saved his life, something which served to support his first impressions. He still saw Pintura as a green kid, making him feel that someone depended on him. Advising on the perils and pitfalls of a town like Las Cruces gave him an unfamiliar feeling of consequence.

'There's still some stuff for you to see, boy,' Book said, and Pintura smiled inwardly at the display of enthusiasm. The guard nodded to his colleagues. He settled brief introductions, and Pintura learned where each man was posted, the hour and minute they were signed on. He took in every feature of the bank's magnitude, his interest being interpreted as boyish curiosity.

'Could be vultures flyin' up there,' he said, ogling the high ceiling.

'Hah, could be,' Book replied with a happy chuckle, his unwitting complicity exactly as Fausto Salt had imagined it would be. Book said that they change shifts at six o'clock, and Pintura replied that he'd be back, that he wanted to see more.

'Yeah, sure, but not so much excitement this time eh?' the guard agreed with more foolish laughing.

Pintura returned to the hotel with a tale of everything going to plan. He told Fausto Salt that the bank doors were closed at four, that guards had coffee at five when all the customers and staff had left. Book was off duty at six, and the manager always waited until the night relief arrived before he too made his way home.

Salt listened to the information with a smirk of satisfaction. He sat thinking awhile, but then took to pacing the room. There were still hours to go, and they would go slowly. A familiar thirst burned in Salt's throat, but he appreciated the need for caution. The only one of them who could move freely about the town streets was Pintura, but due to his youthful appearance, he looked wrong for the next and immediate chore Salt had in mind for him.

'Hey Geth,' he said, yielding to temptation. 'Go get me a bottle of whiskey. I've got a throat that's drier'n a cork leg. Pay cash, an' for God's sake make sure they don't think it's for you.'

Jack Calveron elbowed his way to the long bar of the Paraiso. A few heads turned as he made his way forward, and he recognized the crooked figure of Charlie Wei as one of them.

The old Chinaman set his head on one side, gave the sheriff, then Jack an inscrutable stare. 'You've got a nerve, mister,' he said, edging sideways to get between Jack and the bar. 'You figure you're some big thing in this town? You figure you can ride in, do as you damn well please?'

Jack glared at him, not sure what to say other than to disagree. Lewis Berry attempted to intervene, but there was an indignation running hotly through Wei, and he wasn't for shutting up.

'You held a gun on me, goddamnit . . . near broke

my hand. You marched the sheriff out of here like a desperado. What are you up to, mister?'

'As I recall I was protecting myself from you.' Jack spoke quietly, but his eyes were piercing. He didn't feel like explaining or justifying himself. 'My business is with the sheriff, and it doesn't concern you, so button it,' he offered.

'He's right, Charlie.' Berry reached out, catching Wei's arm in time to prevent him laying a hand on Jack. 'You're riled because he roughed you up a little, but that was your fault. Don't do it again. He's a man who fights bears . . . Weaver's bears. I've seen him do it.'

Wei's expression slowly opened, his eyes more interested. 'You mean you've tangled with 'em?'

'Yeah, we sure have, Charlie.' Berry related a brief account of the shooting and the fight in the mine shaft. He told it despite a protest from Jack that it was an overstatement. Nevertheless, when he was done, Wei's manner was discernibly calmed.

'Well I might've been wrong about you . . . might've,' Wei said. Then he shuffled about, took another less antagonistic look at Jack. 'I guess you know what you're doing, if you're going up against Erskine Weaver. An' *his* enemy's *our* friend, or something like that. But I'd still like to know what's between you an' our sheriff.'

'Yeah, I just bet you would,' Jack muttered, as the barkeep pushed a bottle and glasses within easy reach.

Charlie Wei took willingly to the pouring. It was a

long time since there'd been someone like Jack Calveron in Las Cruces, and Wei wanted some of the credit for keeping him there, some of the glory if there was going to be any. Wei had respect for the sheriff, knew that Berry had done much good for the town. But there had always been a weakness. Wei couldn't define it, just felt that Jack Calveron had something to do with it.

As the three men drank, the side door opened and a young man entered. He walked straight for the bar, and almost immediately a frown wrinkled Wei's forehead. The man he observed was young, hardly into his teens, but the old Chinaman linked him with something else. Maybe another place or another time, definitely something that bothered him.

'You ever seen that feller before?' Wei said, still watching the young man as he approached the bar.

Berry squinted through the smoke haze, while Jack took a sideways step to see where Wei was looking.

Gethin Pintura took a bottle of whiskey from the barkeep, paid, nodded civilly and turned to leave. There was something familiar about him, the handsome, dark features. He walked with a light step, and though he didn't carry a gun, Jack was placing one there.

'He's one of the bunch who held up the bank,' Jack said. He remembered the eyes, the flashing murderous look from low across the neck of a running horse, a gun that blazed at him because he was standing in the way. 'They've given him a haircut an' a scrub, but that's him. Lawmen are good at remembering faces. It's been known to keep 'em alive.'

Berry muttered an oath, snapped his glass back on the counter. He made a move for his gun, but Jack's hand was whipping down, closing tight around his wrist before he had a chance to draw.

'He's bought that whiskey for someone else. If he doesn't return with it, they'll clear town within ten minutes,' Jack rasped. 'We watch him, find out what he's up to, who else is involved. And remember to tell me the next time you decide to pull that Colt. I might misunderstand your intention,' he added sternly.

'They're after robbing another bank most likely,' Berry said. 'Do you think they're crazy enough to try again . . . so soon?'

Jack shrugged. 'Why not? It looks like they're crazy enough to come back.'

Berry watched Pintura retreat through the side door. 'They must be staying here in town, just keeping low an' somewhere close, I'll wager,' he said quietly.

'Yeah, so we keep a close watch. Your office is sited to give a broad view, and it's a natural place for you to be, or *was*,' he told Berry. 'You go and let Raphaela know where you are, that you're still in one piece. Maybe she can rustle up some food.' Jack downed his drink and pushed the bottle in front of Wei. 'You, Chinaman, can go and advise the mayor to ready a posse . . . a reliable one. We want to confront them, not go on a wild goose chase.'

Wei poured himself an expedient measure of whiskey. 'I was hoping to stay here an' watch, in case the youngster comes back,' he said.

'You only want to watch that bottle. Just go see the mayor, then meet me across the street. You'll be a sort of deputy.'

Jack rolled his eyes with incredulity as he left the saloon. Everything was a far cry from what he had in mind when he was banged up in the Redrock stockade. A town called Las Cruces was in danger of being cleaned up by a dishonest sheriff, a stove-up old Chinaman and an ex-jail bird.

17

Goose Hollister rode hard, pulling off the trail to the Weaver mine with his horse panting and flecked with foam. With the horse ground-hitched, he ran straight to the cabin, pushing against the door without knocking.

Erskine Weaver struggled to his feet. As he grabbed for a Colt that was hanging on the arm of his chair, the light fell on his face, accentuating the grey grimace of pain.

'What's happened? Are you OK?' Hollister gasped.

'No. I mean, yes, but I'll live. We've had some trouble,' Weaver muttered sullenly. 'But that can wait. What did you find out in town?'

'It's the same bunch all right,' Hollister replied. 'They're booked into the Prosperity Hotel, an' they've been takin' a look at the bank. The big Las Cruces one.'

Weaver's eyes narrowed. He listened without interruption, then nodded in understanding as he was told about Fausto Salt's visit to the store and the information Hollister had drawn out of Pat Fairley.

'They're going to cold-cock the guards with a lousy potion?' Weaver said in amazement as he paced the room. 'Goddamnit, there's half a goddamn fortune in that bank if they can get away with it.'

Weaver took a deep breath, gritting his teeth against the hurt in his side. He couldn't, wouldn't stand by and allow a gang of nonentities to move in. The way he saw it, the assets of the Las Cruces Depository remained his, to transfer if and when *he* chose.

'Round up everyone,' he decided. 'When I say the word, I want every man to ride, even if they've got to be lifted into the saddle. If those turkeys want to rob the depository let 'em. Nobody ought to be a gainer by their own wrongdoing. So we'll take it off 'em.'

Hollister grinned meanly, muttered his appreciation of Weaver's irony and headed off to the workmen's cabins. He'd yet to learn about the visit of Jack Calveron and the sheriff, but it wouldn't have made a difference. Erskine Weaver knew exactly what he wanted and had the means to get it. Any man who tried to thwart him would soon be stepping off the Catwalk Bridge.

The men had stopped working. They were mostly sprawled on their bunks, tending their wounds. Hollister cursed at the pungency, sucked air through his teeth at seeing the smashed faces and purpling eyes. He saw a man with his shoulder strapped, another with an arm that was obviously broken, another with a shattered jaw. He learned of Weaver's two guards being shot, the subsequent violence in the mine tunnel. It seemed incredible that two men could have been responsible for such havoc. Hollister then recalled the stranger who had ridden into town with Sheriff Berry.

A scowl worked across Hollister's malicious features. To rub out the dangerous troublemaker would not only make staying alive a tad more certain, but earn him respect and gratitude from the men, and probably a big bonus from Weaver. So, tonight or early tomorrow, Goose Hollister would be seeking an opportunity to get rid of Jack Calveron.

It was approaching first dark, the snow-covered peaks of the San Andreas Mountains still glowing under late rays of the sun. Along the main street of Las Cruces, long shadows were thrown from one side to the other. At ten minutes before five o'clock, there was already a discernible chill in the air, an uneasy silence, as though nature itself was steeled in readiness for looming trouble.

From behind a slatted blind in the sheriff's office, Jack Calveron cursed quietly and took a small step back. From an angle across the street, he was watching as the big double doors of the depository swung open.

'What . . . the . . . hell?' he said slowly, as he saw Gethin Pintura enter the bank, the doors closing quickly behind him. 'What the hell?' he repeated, dropping his hands and turning to face Charlie Wei and Lewis Berry.

133

'What's going on? What have you seen?' Berry asked, stepping up to take a look for himself.

'That young feller's just gone in,' Jack remarked, sounding as though he doubted what he'd seen. 'Who the hell opened up? One of the guards?'

Berry cleared his throat. 'Sure makes robbing a bank a lot easier,' he replied drily. 'But if Forge has posted men at every likely exit out of town, they won't get far. Not this time.'

'And when it's over?' Jack enquired.

'I gave you my word, didn't I? We'll head for Tucson.'

Jack didn't think there was need to say more. He was aware of Charlie Wei's curious stare, but held it was Berry who must do the explaining. Sheriff Lewis Berry who had to start telling about the lies, and end with telling the truth.

18

It was Minty Book who opened the bank's double doors to Gethin Pintura's knock. He stared at the young man, concern wrinkling his broad face. 'You shouldn't be here. The bank's closed,' he said. 'No one's allowed in after closing time. We got strict instructions.'

'I know, Minty, I'm real sorry,' Pintura apologized. 'I was goin' to get coffee along the street, but there was some sort o' ruckus, an' I'd been told to stay clear of anythin' like that. I thought it best to come straight here.'

'Yeah, you did the right thing. You'd better come in then.'

Pintura stepped past Book, immediately looked all around him. 'Wow!' he exclaimed, keeping up the pretence of wonder. 'It's even bigger'n I remembered.'

A guard made a move towards his Colt then relaxed, moving on when he recognized Pintura.

'I won't cause any trouble. I promise,' Pintura said lightly. 'You won't even know I'm here, except maybe to fix coffee for you an' the others.'

'Are you always this helpful, kid?'

'No, not always. Pa says not, anyway. Hah, truth is, I wouldn't mind some myself,' Pintura said, adding a cheeky smile. 'When the next shift comes on, we can take a look at the town, like you said. I've been lookin' forward to that, Minty.'

Pintura knew where to find the small scullery at the rear of the building. It had been built to cater for the basic needs of both day and night time staff, but recently improved for important and influential customers.

When he was certain he wasn't going to be interrupted for a minute or so, Pintura took the sleeping draught purchased by Fausto Salt, prised off the small cork and tipped it into the steaming pot. His heart was racing, and he could feel sweat running between his shoulder blades. He wasn't so much scared as tense. It wasn't often he was up to no good while surrounded by a small army of guards. Then there was the possibility of the tranquillizer not working, or that if it did, it wouldn't be for long enough. It might work on prize bulls and work horses, but who knew about its effectiveness on men? Eagerly stirring the coffee, he offered up some cruel silent curses, then set out the cans on a table in the centre of the room.

It was a few minutes off five o'clock, and Minty Book came in just before the rest of the guards. Two of them nodded a greeting to Pintura, another gave Book a look of open concern. The Las Cruces Depository had a strict code of conduct, rules for its employees. Book risked instant dismissal if the presence of Gethin Pintura became known to the manager.

'Kid ain't doin' any harm,' Book said defensively. 'If you fellers will keep your mouths shut, no one need know about it.'

The men drank their coffee. Pintura sat watching each man sip at the loaded brew, nervously waiting for a sign that it was taking effect. The minutes dragged, and one man set down his can and fumbled for his makings. Another followed suit. With their coffees drained, each man sat and quietly smoked.

One of them smothered a yawn. 'I feel so goddamn tired, I could sleep for the Union. What the hell did you make that coffee with, kid?' he asked, innocently.

Pintura smiled in return. 'I was hopin' it weren't too strong for you,' he started. 'My pa always said, a cup o' coffee should be well built . . . strong enough to bring down a proddy buffler.'

'Yeah, not a goddamn herd,' another of the guards slurred, stiffling a yawn.

It was then that it came to them, the realization of what was really wrong. Minty Book lurched to his feet, stood swaying and shaking his big head in an effort to clear the fugginess.

'You did put somethin' in the coffee, you little

runt,' a guard rasped, making a move for his holstered Colt. But before he had time to raise it, the weapon slid from his useless fingers. The other men rose and tried to find their footing. One stumbled, made a grab for the table only to tip it on its side.

Book staggered forward, snarling, reached out to grab at Pintura. His outstretched hand pawed at Pintura's face, his other hand grappled his shoulder. 'Hey, kid?' he mumbled, 'What sort of stunt you pullin'? Somebody set you up, is that it? You in some kind o' trouble?'

'No, ox brain, you are. An' I remember tellin' you not to lay your maws on me.' Pintura shook free of the big man's grasp, moving to drag the Colt from Book's holster. He flipped it in his hand, holding the barrel as he raised it up. He brought the Colt cracking down and Book grunted once and dropped. He rolled on the floor, clutching his head, trying to look up until Pintura hit him again. Quickly Pintura swung on the others. One by one he clubbed them with the barrel of the Colt as they stood bewildered and defenceless. When he was done he stood in the centre of the room, breathing heavy, venomous black eyes flicking from one unconscious guard to the next.

The sleeping physic had been effective, and Pintura had acted quickly, but there had been a lot of wrong noise from the scullery. The door flew open and a dark-suited man stood there. He looked on speechless until Pintura turned the Colt in his hand

and pointed it directly between his fearful eyes.

'Good evenin', Mr Manager. Open your mouth, make a sound an' you'll be swimmin' with these fish.' Pintura stepped over a comatose body, pushed the barrel of Book's Colt hard up under the bank manager's chin. 'Take a step back an' turn around,' he instructed. 'Move slowly to the front door, open it a mite, and don't try anythin' stupid. Do as you're told, an' you might get to go home tonight.'

Terrified, almost unable to breathe, the manager walked back along the corridor, crossing by the tellers' cages to the front door. He eased the bolts free, pushed the door open an inch or so and then stepped back.

With the minutes ticking away, Fausto Salt and Wallace Trench had their mounts saddled and ready to ride. They jogged along the quiet shadowy street until they drew near the bank. They led Pintura's horse, leaving it loose hitched with their own at a corner where an alleyway ran off the main street. They walked back casually along the walkway, pausing for a discreet look around before stepping through the doors of the bank.

The two men drew their Colts, nodded an acknowledgement at Pintura as they pushed the bank manager ahead of them.

'Open the safe ... the big fancy one,' Salt said fiercely. 'Don't take long, else I'll shut you in there when we leave.'

With guns at his back, threatenings of death provoking him, the manager hastened to obey Salt. Nervously, he scrabbled at the safety plate. He inserted the key in the lock, taking a moment to dab at the sweat breaking across his forehead. He looked up once, meeting the impatient, hostile stares of Pintura and Salt. With his jaw hurting and his heart pounding, he jiggled the key and rotated it. He was scared, bewildered at how easily Pintura had overpowered the guards. He was reeling at the suddenness of it all and, knowing they would surely kill him, his breathing became laboured. The inner bolt gave way, and his legs buckled as he swung the heavy door open.

Pintura grunted something at Salt and Trench as he stepped forward. He pushed the Colt into his trouser belt, grasped the fallen bank manager and pulled him back off the ground. He crooked his right arm around the man's neck, gave one hard, jerking twist until the resistance broke, then he straightened with a step back.

'What the hell did you do that for?' Salt demanded.

'To stop him squealin' before we're done.'

'You're some piece o' work, Gethin. Whoever it was dubbed you Copperhead, knew a thing or two,' Salt observed. 'Now come an' help unpack this before the changeover guard arrives.'

Pintura, Salt and Trench started to clean the safe out. They gathered up green canvas sacks of big denomination coin and bundles of folding dollars.

Wanting everything the safe contained, they worked quickly and in silence, listening for any sound of forewarning from the street outside.

19

From his vantage point Jack Calveron watched the approach of Salt and Trench, saw them pause a moment on the walkway outside of the depository. His heart thumped, when, just for an instant he thought he met their eyes across the street when Salt had a look around.

As the two men slipped inside the building, Jack glanced back to Lewis Berry who seemed to suffering from a brief melancholy. 'You know there should be some coffee here somewhere,' he said. 'I could use one right now.'

'No time,' Charlie Wei returned. 'I guess this might come in handy,' he added, getting the feel of a scattergun. 'We'll take 'em as they come out. They'll be running but they won't reach their horses.'

'Yeah, that's right.' Aware that it had to end in a gun fight, Jack nodded, suddenly recalling one thing that an inmate of Redrock had told him. 'Most bank bandits don't think ahead,' he'd said. 'Most of 'em don't know that carryin' loot's like draggin' a mud wagon. It slows you down some'.

But this gang were already cited for murder, so there was no other way. The moment they were all clear of the bank, they'd be ready for the first sign of trouble, would begin blasting.

Jack hefted his big .44 Colt, turned the chamber to check the loads. He lifted his eyes to see Berry now doing the same, giving a thought to Leo Forge who had men posted in the chance event of a bank robber getting clear. Jack had never thought his mission to bring Berry to book would come to this. But from the moment he'd closed in on Las Cruces, he should have. He shook the thoughts clear, looking back across the street to the depository. The men presently relieving it of its funds knew what to expect if they got caught. Eluding an incapable posse was one thing; caught in a volley of concentrated fire from a sheriff's office was another. Yeah. Robbing one bank's stupid enough. Robbing two's disastrous, he thought.

'Berry,' Jack started, 'as soon as we're out of here, you go right. I'll go left. Charlie, you're taking centre stage with that cannon, but don't stand in the doorway,' he commanded. 'An' remember they won't be negotiating a surrender. They'll be cutting loose the moment they clap eyes on us.'

Jack stepped to the door. He was about to move out to the walkway when Berry, uttering a loud curse, held up his arm. Further down the street, lamps were already being lit, and in the glow from one of them the figure of a girl could be seen approaching.

'Goddamnit, it's Raph. She's bringing supper. She's going to walk right by that bank, an' get caught in the middle.'

Raphaela came on carrying a basket covered with a cloth. She was looking up, and her face could now be seen clearly. She neared the bank, the heels of her shoes clicking on the walkway. Not wanting to make the drama worse, Jack bit back on his own fear. He saw the doors of the bank open slightly and guessed the raiders were appraising the street before they dared to venture out. It was too late to call a warning, too late to make any move without endangering Raphaela.

I'd make a run for it now. Girl coming, but coast's clear enough, Jack thought. As if at his bidding, the bank doors opened wider and one man and then another stepped out on to the walkway.

They were level with Raphaela and she stopped, turning to stare. She saw that each of them carried a big canvas sack in one hand a Colt in the other. Her eyes darted to the heavy features of Fausto Salt, then Wallace Trench. Then she saw Gethin Pintura as he, too, emerged from the building.

The realization of what was happening froze Raphaela to the walkway. Fascinated and frightened, she found her gaze locked with that of the young man. She saw the lust and brutality in the black pits of his eyes, and gasped. She cried out in fear but no sound came.

Pintura grinned, his lips curling back in recognition.

She was the same girl he had seen that morning, the girl he'd watched from the hotel window. He absorbed her looks, the lines of her body, and the warnings of Fausto Salt fell on deaf ears.

'Gethin, let's get out of here. Gethin,' Salt was yelling harshly.

Pintura moved fast. His reached out and grabbed Raphaela by the wrist. His fingers dug into her flesh and the basket of food spilled across the walkway.

'For God's sake, Gethin, what the hell are you doin'? Let her go,' Salt yelled out again.

Wallace Trench started to run. They were out of the bank and they had the cash. It was ride off or stay and get killed. Running for the corner, he looked back, saw that Pintura still held the girl and Salt was cursing him. There was little friendship between them the three of them now. It had suddenly become every man for himself.

Across the street, a masked man moved out of the shadows. A second man emerged, a third and a fourth. Further down towards the corner, more similarly disguised figures were closing in.

Goose Hollister gave the order for the shooting to start, and impatient guns crashed out a deafening fusillade. Behind Hollister, safely withdrawn, Erskine Weaver stood watching. He nodded, made balls of his fists and smirked.

Weaver wasn't over concerned that the sheriff's office was close, set almost opposite the depository. He was employing enough weaponry to settle the hash of Lewis Berry and company. He was worried about Jack Calveron, but his overriding concern was the big bank's cash reserves, and whoever was attempting to steal it.

Under his instructions, his men had delayed their assault until the outlaws stepped in to the street. They saw the money sacks that Salt and the other two dragged out through the big doors, grinned with satisfaction as that part of the raid was being carried out for them. All they had to do now was to gun down the would-be thieves and take over the loot.

Hollister fired first. His bullet caught Wallace Trench in the meat of the shoulder, spinning him back against the wall of the bank. Trench shouted that he was hit, then ducked, diving for cover as other guns blasted into the echoes of following gunfire. Another bullet shattered Trench's knee. He made a desperate attempt to reach the corner, dragging himself along on his belly. He knew he was alone, with lead biting lumps from the walkway, smacking into the brick walls of the bank.

'Fausto!' he cried out, twisting back to see what was going on. 'I'm hit, Fausto. Help me.' But he saw that Salt and Pintura were already pulling back; Pintura dragging the girl to the safety of the depository.

From the shelter of the bank, Salt and Pintura dropped the cash sacks. Salt turned to Raphaela. 'Step back outside an' you'll probably end up in a dozen pieces,' he warned.

The two men returned fire, but in their haste it was indiscriminate and ineffective. But, taking up the guards' Winchester rifles, they settled, raking the walkways, doors and windows of buildings opposite with lethal gunfire. One man pitched forward through a shattered glass door, another dropped his gun when he was hit, clutching his stomach before falling from the walkway.

Trench took a shallow, agonized breath. Using his elbows for support, he grasped his Colt in both hands. He took aim at a big man who appeared to be leading the bunch and squeezed the trigger, determinedly. Grinding his teeth in pain, he watched the man double over, collapsing sideways as if to sleep in the dirt of the street.

Almost instantaneously, every gun homed in on the prone figure of Wallace Trench. He rolled over and pressed his back to the clapboards. Bullets thumped into him, hot and deep to the vitals of his upper body. With his vision glazing over, he fired out across the street at the hazy figures that appeared to be coming towards him. Blood erupted from his mouth, seeped from the holes in his chest and he was beyond feeling. The Colt was empty and he let it drop. 'Sons o' bitches. All o' you,' he rasped. Slowly, his body toppled sideways, slumping lifeless to the blood-smeared walkway.

20

A discordant yell erupted from Erskine Weaver's men, but short lived, when Salt and Pintura increased their rate of fire from the broken window of the depository. A man ran to help a fallen colleague, but he too went down, kicking and thrashing when a bullet ripped low into his side.

Goose Hollister cursed in anger. Wallace Trench's final bullet had hit him in the hip, lodged itself deep in sinew. He twisted himself one way, looking at the cover, the back up of where he'd come from, then ahead towards the bank. He pushed with his good leg, raised himself to fire despondently at the shattered windows. A returning shot hit him high in the chest. 'Goddamn sittin' duck,' he groaned, forcing an agonized grin. But the bleak remark worked like an invite and brought another bullet hammering home. Who the hell are they? he wondered, as his face crushed into the hard-packed runnels of the street.

With a plentiful supply of guns and ammunition,

Salt and Pintura continued to pour a relentless hail of lead from the depository. But the fall of Hollister was a sign to the rest of the Weaver bunch to scatter, to retreat into the deep shadows. Leaderless, and with bullets spitting at their heels, another man tripped in fear, went down hard against the raised walkway.

Erskine Weaver held out a plated .44 Navy Colt. He was maddened, firing frustratedly as he ran into the open, 'Goddamn you useless hams,' he bellowed, heading for the depository. He continued cursing the incompetence of his own men, then the men inside the bank. He couldn't be beaten now. He'd snatch the money and get clear of Las Cruces, clear of the ruse of a goddamn dry silver mine. With what he'd already got stashed away, he'd have the collateral to set himself up in comfort someplace else . . . *anywhere* else. Yes that was it. He'd start over, and for the shortest moment, images of Red River paddle steamers and Denver dance halls swam dreamily around him.

'They've got Raphy. They've got her in the bank.' Lewis Berry decided to make a break for the door and Jack had to reach out and grab him, pull him back. The sheriff cursed again with helplessness. 'They'll kill her unless I get over there.'

They'll kill her the moment you do, Jack thought, but didn't say so. 'It's too late for that sort of heroics. Besides, they haven't got the time to harm her. Right now they've got other stuff to worry about.'

As if in agreement, Charlie Wei took hold of Berry's arm, glancing at Jack while the firing across the street continued.

'Have you seen anyone out there you recognize?' Jack asked of the Chinaman.

'Yeah, it's Weaver an' his crew.' Wei nodded. 'That means they got a sniff o' this bank robbery, an' they're goin' to do just what they did to me an' the mine,' he added soberly.

'Yeah, I heard. Are you thinking we should let 'em?'

Wei looked surprised. 'I think if we let 'em shoot it out, Raphaela's liable to stop a bullet, stray or otherwise. She's not plumb in the middle, but she's caught.'

'I know. That's why I'm going to take a look inside that bank while they continue waging war on each other,' Jack said. 'Very soon, when he realizes what's going on, Leo Forge will bring his men here to keep you company. Meantime, you keep an eye on the sheriff. Don't let him go barging out there trying to tackle them on his own. Can you do that?'

'What goes on in that street's my responsibility,' Berry intervened. 'I'm still the sheriff of Las Cruces.'

'Were,' Jack countered with a nod towards Wei. 'Just keep him here.'

With that, Jack hurried out the back door into the yard. He eased himself over the fence at the rear, and dropped down. Keeping low and out of line of sight, he crossed the main street, using the darkness, weaving around the back lanes until he reached the garbage pens behind the depository.

He couldn't see, and didn't expect there to be, any entry at ground level. But there was a water tank supported by four cross-beamed stilts and he climbed it to the roof. He saw glass panes glinting darkly in a skylight and edged his way carefully forward. Gunfire continued to sound from the street below, and he clearly heard Erskine Weaver's desperate commands to his men.

It was a double skylight, and through one side he looked down into the bank's materials storage area. The other half of the sloping light was almost directly above the tellers' cages and the long shiny counter. He cursed silently at the sight of the safe with its door wide open, the body of the manager crumpled neatly in front of it. By one of the large windows at the front of the building, he saw the huddled figure of Fausto Salt. On the other side of the big doors, he could see Raphaela and Gethin Pintura.

Hoping and guessing correctly that it wouldn't be locked due to the bank being guarded twenty-four hours a day, he put both hands to the casement. The hinged skylight opened easy enough, but it creaked loudly and Jack held his breath, cringing as he let it back down.

Salt turned to look up at the sound. 'Geth. I think someone's up on the roof,' he called out.

Pintura had heard the noise, but he'd been too intent on street fighting to look up. 'Maybe that big gold eagle out front's got a mate.'

'Won't be so goddamn funny if it drops on your

head,' Salt snapped back, ducking as more bullets took out shards of glass from the corners of the windows. He rammed fresh loads into his gun's cylinder, standing up to empty it with vicious epithets. 'You shouldn't have grabbed the girl. She's no use to us,' he returned to Pintura. 'We could've made it to the horses and been out of here. Perhaps I should've let Trench geld you.'

'This is the use of her,' Pintura snarled in reply. He looked at Raphaela's frightened face, then stood up, and to one side of the window. 'You, out there.' The firing was now more ragged, and his voice cut through it. 'You know we've got the girl. So back off, or she'll never leave here alive.'

'Do as you goddamn please. You'll be saving us the trouble,' Weaver snorted a few moments later. The girl was the sheriff's stepdaughter, but apart from the town losing a pretty face, her well-being made little difference to Weaver's end game.

Pintura spat. He was puzzled, figuring the guns out front were defending their bank as well as their townsfolk. Now he sensed the reality, and a burning anger seized him. 'Do as you goddamn please,' Weaver had mocked, and Pintura's finger tightened eagerly on the trigger.

21

Jack took the chance of not being hit as he quickly opened the skylight again. He took a breath and swung his legs through; in one continuous movement, gripped the casement frame, lowered his body and dropped to the floor below. His knees jarred and he went to ground rolling, but then rising and clutching his big Colt.

He saw Pintura with a gun aimed at Raphaela, heard the warning yell from Salt. But Jack's concern was for the girl's safety. He didn't have time to defend himself against Salt and there was no time to warn Pintura.

Jack's big Colt boomed inside the confines of the bank. Pintura dropped his gun, spun away yelling in shock. Fausto Salt opened fire, and Jack felt the hammer of a bullet in his side, low across his ribs. He lurched to one side, went into a crouch and fired again. Fausto Salt took the bullet high in his leg, gasping with pain, collapsing back against the wall alongside the bank's double doors.

'The next bullet will kill one of you,' Jack shouted. 'Drop your guns.'

Pintura leaned back away from the window and clutched his arm. Fury blazed in his black eyes as the blood seeped across his fingers. His teeth ground in anger and he dropped his gun, watching bitterly as Raphaela stumbled quickly towards Jack.

'No, you're in my way,' Jack yelled, moving to keep Raphaela in the clear.

But it was a chance for Salt, and he took it. He was still holding on to his Colt, and as Raphaela ran towards Jack, he fired.

The bullet ripped across the top of Jack's shoulder, and the force knocked him backwards and off balance. Raphaela screamed, Salt turned for the door with Pintura at his heels and Jack was shaking his head in confusion.

Running from the sheriff's office, to voice his own challenge, Lewis Berry decided to test the nerve and allegiance of Charlie Wei. 'Where's my stepdaughter, you son-of-a-bitch?' he bellowed.

Weaver's response was a bullet that was meant for Fausto Salt. But it found Berry, collapsing him into the street from the edge of the walkway.

Charlie Wei threw down his scattergun and limped straight out to the stricken sheriff. He knelt, looked up alertly then back down at his hands that were already damp with blood. 'My job to look out for you,' he mumbled. 'You die, I die.'

Salt kept running until a bullet shattered his back. 'Goddamn you, Gethin,' he seethed as he fell. 'You an' your goddamn bean.' His legs lifted once and his heels kicked street dirt, then more bullets hit him and he lay still.

Charlie Wei raised his head again. 'I'd have liked one o' them bullets to have been mine,' he sighed. 'Now perhaps someone can get the doc, if he ain't too busy.'

Pintura gulped with fear. He looked around for Trench and Salt, but he knew they were dead. He ran along the walkway, dodging and weaving, keeping to the deeper shadows best he could. But the strain of the hour and being hit had started to weaken him. He saw the lights of the grub house and a milling group of inquisitive townfolk who were keeping a safe distance from the shooting.

Pintura grabbed for breath, his heart pounding, his lungs beginning to burn. His head was swimming; the lights, the buildings, the horses tethered along the street, seemed to melt one into the other. He saw a doorway ahead, a partly open door that might offer refuge from the angry guns that pursued him. He stumbled inside, gasping for respite, hardly noticing the surrounding pall of shaded red light.

A moment later, he looked up into the girl's pale face, caught the drift of cheap perfume.

'They'll kill me if they find me,' he said, fighting for more awareness.

'Then it's not your lucky day.' The girl spoke through hurt lips, and Pintura remembered her voice.

*

Erskine Weaver watched in incredulity as Lewis Berry went down, cursed a moment later as Fausto Salt died kicking dirt in the street. When Charlie Wei called out for help, he grunted, pulled back the hammer of his Colt and started towards the depository.

The bank robbers might have fled, but the money was conveniently packed. All he had to do was drag the sacks along the walkway and, using their mounts as pack horses, saddle up and ride. Or die in the attempt, was his more probable, rational thought.

As his men went after Pintura, Weaver started his run for the bank. He was considering the sack that Wallace Trench had been carrying, when Jack Calveron emerged on the walkway in front of him. For a long moment they faced each other, Weaver wound up, his face set in anticipation, Jack with an injured shoulder, chilly with nerves. Both men held their Colts at their sides.

'I asked you once before, feller, what the hell do you want?' Weaver managed.

'I told you: I've got a job to do. You're in the way . . . making it difficult.'

To Raphaela, inside the bank, crouched back and well out of the way, the seconds that passed were like an eternity. She had seen the likes of Jack Calveron before. The tough ones with cause and reason behind them, if not always the law. But this man was something else, and determined to take her stepfather away. Yet she couldn't deny her feelings for him.

'You know that assay business would never have

proved anything. So what the hell does a man like you want with me . . . with bank robbing and street gunfighting?' Weaver demanded of Jack.

'I think you've just put a bullet into what it is I wanted . . . what I came here for,' Jack said. 'An' now you're headed somewhere I don't want you to go.'

Weaver licked his mouth, gripped the Colt in a palm that was greasing up with sweat. 'You want the money for yourself? Is that it?'

Jack gave a tired, half smile. 'No. I couldn't give a fig. But that doesn't mean you're going through the doors of this bank.'

For the shortest moment, Weaver was lost in thought as he tried to work out the implication of Jack's words. Then, very swiftly he brought up his Colt. The resignation of failure blazed in his eyes, a tremor of impending death running through him as he pulled the trigger.

He knew he was outgunned. Everything was too late and he was too slow. He was recalling the death of his two gun-hands at the mine as the dreadful punch of Jack's bullet struck him. He had a last look at the bright blue stare that bade him farewell. 'Why—?' he started, but never finished.

22

Leo Forge had deployed his posse to every exit from town likely to see a fast running horse. By the time he'd managed to rally everyone together the shooting was over. As soon as the Weaver men who hadn't already fled were rounded up, he headed for the depository.

'It looks like your father's hurt bad,' he said, putting his hand on Raphaela's shoulder. The girl was pale and shaky. She was sickened by the noise, the cordite that stung her eyes, the men lying dead in the street, the thought that Berry might die.

Jack was kneeling beside the wounded man, saw the blood-soaked shirt. 'Your Chinee friend's gone to find out where McKrew is,' he said. 'It's not much more than a flesh wound. You must've recovered from worse.'

Berry raised his hand weakly to acknowledge Jack's opinion. 'Just in case I don't,' he murmured, 'there's someone you ought to know about. He's holed up in Santa Rita or Mimbres. His name's—'

'Yeah,' Jack interrupted. 'There's always going to be someone, holed up somewhere. Let's leave it like that . . . them thinking one day I'll turn up.'

Jack got slowly to his feet. Looking now at Forge, he saw the man's face taut with anxiety and weariness. 'Reckon that's it then,' he offered in mutual concern.

'I don't know where it leaves us though . . . the town.' Forge cleared his throat, gave a tired grin. 'Thanks for clearing the place up. As for your remark about not being such a good shot as you used to be? From what I've seen an' heard, I'm glad I never crossed you five years ago. As it is, I guess you'll be leaving us . . . moving on.'

If there was anything to what the mayor said, Jack had the appreciation of the town. And he could have the name of a man he hunted if he wanted it. 'Not until I know where I'm going,' he answered, returning the weary smile.

'What do you mean by that?' Raphaela asked. 'We live from day to day waiting to see what you intend to do? After all this, isn't there any pardon in you?'

'Yes. But there's part of me that regrets he's the man you claim him to be.'

Raphaela understood, struggled against her frustration. 'Well he would have kept his promise. He would have gone back to Tucson and accepted a prison sentence for what he did. He probably still will. He's an honourable man,' she maintained evenly.

'But he wasn't always. Let's not pretend. Besides, I

just said I didn't know where I was going.'

'Have you changed your mind?'

'I think I might have done.'

'Are you going to tell me?'

'If there's somewhere a little less demanding,' Jack said. 'And it's no one else's business.'

A minute or so later, Raphaela sat in her stepfather's chair at his desk in the sheriff's office.

Jack shut the door to the street, let his shoulders sag in respite. 'Back on the trail out of Las Cruces. Do you remember I told you why I couldn't turn the other cheek?' he asked.

Raphaela nodded. 'Yes, of course I do. You also said, you were tired of listening to my "churchy mores".'

'Yes, well. Anyway, I did get to thinking of an option . . . something I'd ride on for. Like, if Berry was manager of the Santa Cruces Depository, would I have accepted a wagonload of dollars?'

'Huh, that's a tad unlikely. He's never been worth more than a plugged nickel.'

'I know. So I kind of decided to take his stepdaughter, instead.'

Raphaela gave Jack an enquiring look, then pulled open the bottom drawer of the desk. 'Wheeew, that's all right then,' she said with a warm, quiet smile. 'For a moment I was worried you were going to say you'd settle for a bag of this goddamn coffee.'